T
Dy
Tho
Murders

For Stevie, Siân and Danny

The
Dylan
Thomas
Murders

DAVID N. THOMAS

seren

Seren is the book imprint of
Poetry Wales Press Ltd
Nolton Street, Bridgend, Wales

www.seren-books.com

© David N. Thomas, 2002

ISBN 1-85411-304-6

A CIP record for this title is available from
the British Library

*The publisher works with the financial assistance of the
Arts Council of Wales*

Cover photograph: George Logan

Printed in Plantin by CPD Wales, Ebbw Vale

Fast Forward 1

Out of a bower of red swine
Howls the foul fiend to heel.
I cannot murder, like a fool,
Season and sunshine, grace and girl,
Nor can I smother the sweet waking.

The Sergeant leaned across the table, and switched on the tape machine. "Now then Les, the bloke had his head bashed in, the crows were pulling out his brains like worms."

And Les, still dreaming of topless gypsy dancers, and wondering if he'd caught anything from a tasselled Andalucian nipple dunked in his wine glass, said: "The first time I saw him I was in Miss Hilton's front garden, cutting the heads off in the borders, that's what she asked me to do. A car pulled up, a big red Volvo, with a black roof rack, and National Trust stickers, not local. He got out, there was no-one else in the car with him. He came up the garden path. He had to go past me to reach the cottage but he didn't say a word. Miss Hilton answered the door. 'Stillness,' he said, holding out his hand. 'Acquisitions and Disposals.' I couldn't see her face but she sounded very surprised. 'Good heavens,' she said. They went inside and I carried on in the border.

"Yes, definitely Stillness. No, I didn't catch his first name.

"Ten minutes later, Waldo turned up, angry, black as thunder, nostrils wide like a dog outside the butcher's. He sniffed round the car, not bothering I was there, then he emptied this plastic bag over the windscreen. Jesus, guts everywhere, blood and slime, and big rolls of intestines which he wrapped round the wipers. Then he went to the back of the car, took something from his pocket, and jammed it hard on the exhaust pipe. A rabbit's head, fresh too, by the look of it.

"No, I didn't say anything, it's not my place. We know he's not always right in the head, but we look after him as we can. He's one of us, and that's good enough for me.

"Dylan Thomas? I know nothing about him and Waldo.

"Anyway, Waldo ran off across the fields and I thought I'd better get out of the way, so I went round the back. Next thing, this Stillness was marching across the lawn, shouting and swearing. I told him I knew nothing about it. He threw a punch and I hit him back solid in the stomach, and he went down, just a bag of wind, nothing to him. He fetched up and I fetched the bike. I went up to the square to sit with the lads. He came past later, driving like fury, but I don't know how far he'd have gone with a rabbit's head on the exhaust."

And the Inspector, who'd once known the real Polly Garter down in New Quay, pulled out his notebook and said: "Dylan Thomas wrote wonderful poems."

"Isn't it funny," remarked the Sergeant, "how most poets die young."

"My father said it was the biggest funeral he'd ever been to."

"My auntie says he died of AIDS in New York."

"I believe," said the Inspector, dreaming of a Ferris wheel in which Dylan aficionados turned forever, "that the CIA had him put down."

Between Lamb and Raven

Rachel and I had moved to west Wales into very early retirement. We'd spent the first two weeks unpacking our books. We would start after breakfast with good intent but within minutes we'd each find some old favourite and we'd spend the rest of the day reading. In the very last box, I found a pamphlet, *The Forensic Examination of Stomach Contents*, written by my uncle Jack, sometime a Chief Superintendent. The cover was splattered with faded blood stains, but Jack would never explain how they came to be there, though he wasn't slow to tell you the pamphlet had come first in the King's Essay Competition in 1948.

There have always been policemen in our family. My brother is a detective specialising in Internet fraud. Though my father hadn't actually been a policeman, he'd been a personnel manager at Butlins, which was much the same thing. His cousin Will, the shabbiest man I had ever seen, had been in Special Branch, and collected Victorian typewriters. We didn't talk much about him. He had once seduced my step-mother whilst my father sat sozzled on the sofa downstairs. My step-mother was good at that sort of thing. She'd even worked in a Bloomsbury hotel, renting out rooms to blue movie makers, and starring in one or two herself. "Iesu mawr," she said a few hours before she died, whilst I was wiping her bum, "those boys had willies down to their knees."

Leaving London for the countryside was all very well, Rachel had said, but I would soon need an interest, capital letters, and it was finding my great-uncle's pamphlet that gave me the idea. I had policing in my blood, a good intuitive sense about people, and a sociologist's eye for the quirks of human behaviour.

"How about private investigation?" I said one evening, having searched through Yellow Pages and found a dearth of country gumshoes.

"Good idea," she replied, without losing concentration on the bacon omelette she was making. "You'll be very good at it."

So that night, as enough rain fell for a year and the river burst its banks and took away our seed potatoes, I planned a different kind of future. I rented an office under the town clock in Lampeter, put ads in the papers and filled in a card for the noticeboard at the supermarket. I phoned the local solicitors to tell them I'd started up, and one sent me a good-luck present the next day – a desk, three odd chairs and a wooden filing cabinet containing a photograph of Diana Dors with a pencilled-in moustache. I sat in the office for two weeks and my only callers were the postman with his circulars, and shoppers asking the way to the discount store. Then one day a plump and rosy-cheeked woman came in, whose grey hair swirled round her head like smoke. She was wearing a hand-knitted, bright blue cardigan that waterfalled from her shoulders, stopping within a ragged inch of the top of her black wellington boots. A farmer's wife, I thought. She sat in the chair facing me, folded her arms and leaned across my desk: "Mr Pritchard? Mr Martin Pritchard?"

"How can I help you?"

"They tell me your wife's a poet."

I nodded, too surprised for words.

"You'll need her help to investigate this." She drew out a copy of the *Cambrian News* from her shopping bag. She thumbed through the inside pages, found what she was looking for, folded the paper in half, and edged it across the desk for me to read. I put on my glasses and read the report: a shed had been stolen from a field near the Scadan Coch pub.

"I should be interested in this?"

"It's part of our cultural heritage."

"A shed?" I was incredulous.

"Would you mock the Boat House at Laugharne? The Muse sailed well enough from there."

I picked up the office diary, and made a show of flicking through the pages, distracted by tiny red flames at the front of her mouth. Not lipstick on her teeth, because she wore none. I wondered if her gums were bleeding.

"You won't have much in there," she said.

"Can you meet my terms?"

"Don't you think," she asked, looking scornfully at me, flashing more fire from between her lips, "that the satisfaction of putting the record straight is worth more than money?"

"I'll find the shed, in between other things..."

"Take this." She passed across the desk a double rabbit's paw, stitched back to back with gold and silver thread. "Now, be careful..." She smiled. I stared. She held her smile. I kept on staring, mesmerised by the red dragon etched across her front teeth.

I found out later that she was the only child of a prosperous abattoir owner, and taught moral philosophy at the university.

★ ★ ★

Rachel has a habit of saying: "If you're hungry, go look for a bagel." Fed up with waiting for nothing to happen, I took her advice. I locked the office and drove to Ciliau Aeron. The Scadan Coch was at the end of the village, next to the church. I'd been there many times before, for although we had only just moved in, we'd been holidaying in the area for years.

The landlord was a one-legged, two-fingered Irishman called O'Malley, who'd once been a leading light in the Free Wales Army. He was also part of Ciliau's pink community, which made many local young farmers apprehensive about using the pub. "We're all poofters at heart," he was fond of telling them, "but some of us have the pleasure of it down below as well." Many thought him handsome, but his face was round and his head as bald as a goose egg.

It was usual for only Welsh to be spoken in the bars, and any persistent transgressors were often asked to leave. "There's nothing like a good thirst to help a man find his tongue," O'Malley used to say. He was famous for his prejudice against the English, but he took to them if they had soft voices, blended with the wallpaper and tried to learn Welsh. "What I can't stand," I once heard him say, "is the weekenders, all turbo cars and turbo boats and bloody turbo voices." The pub's pride and joy was a miniature llama called Llewela, who was trained to spit at anyone with a loud English accent.

O'Malley was behind the bar polishing the pumps. I asked for a pint of Brains. He pulled it gently into the glass, placed it on the counter and handed me some olives and a laverbread dip.

"That missing shed," I said. "How long's it been there?"

"First world war, off and on," he replied over his shoulder, as he went across to serve another customer. "Lorry full of turkeys going to market, pulled out of the car park and hit a wagon carrying timber. The village salvaged the turkeys but Dai Fern Hill took the wood and built the shed from it. That's the story, handed down, like."

I dipped another Crinkle in the laverbread and asked: "What was it used for?"

O'Malley passed across some bubble-and-squeak rissoles. "Dai killed his pigs in there. Strung them up by the back feet from the rafter, sharp knife in the neck, and a bucket to catch the blood. They say you could hear the squealing from the top of Surgeon's Hill."

The rissoles were delicious, made with potatoes and wild garlic. When I'd finished, I paid O'Malley, and walked down the road. I soon found the sign for Fern Hill Farm, painted in white on the side of a rusty milk churn. A piece of blue slate on the wooden gate warned: "Loose Dogs. No callers." The gate was chained and padlocked.

I was wondering what to do when Basset the Post arrived, a man so lugubrious that the rims of his sunken eyes seemed to fall down his cheeks and rest on his droopy, always-damp moustache. "Wouldn't go down there, if I were you," he murmured dolefully.

"How d'you deliver the letters, then?"

He nodded towards a wooden box next to the churn. "He don't get much, just bills, and letters from abroad sometimes."

"What's he like?"

"Bitter," said the mournful Basset.

"About what?" I tried to lighten up the question with a smile but Basset wiped it from my face with a melancholic sigh.

"His woman got pregnant by the fertiliser man."

"And?"

"They ran away to Slough."

"And now his shed's gone missing."

"It meant a lot to him, that shed."

I jumped over the gate and walked apprehensively up the track. The trees on either side had not been cut for many years, and their branches intertwined above the track, blocking out much of the daylight. I came to a second gate, also chained, and guarded by something more sinister. A line of dead birds were tied to the top rail with orange baler twine. The three thrushes I cared little about, but it upset me to see the red kite. Someone had broken its neck before tying it to the gate by its legs. Flies were buzzing in and out of its empty eye sockets, whilst little coffee-coloured maggots burrowed through the flesh. As I clambered over, its razor beak caught the inside of my trouser leg and made a small tear.

Another five minutes of walking uphill brought me to the farmhouse. It was a dilapidated building of old Welsh stone, smothered by imperial ivy and climbing roses that reached to the eaves. Ferns had taken root in the gaps between the stones, and a twisted elder grew flag-like from the chimney stack. Pigeons flew in and out of a broken bedroom window, and crows pecked like addicts for the linseed oil in the putty. I relaxed a little as I crossed the yard because I was sure there were no dogs here. The front door was open. An inquisitive sociologist, I had always told my students, should never let a threshold hold him back. I stepped inside.

I found myself in a large room that would have made the turbo-weekenders gasp both with joy and horror. There were two inglenook fires, a slate floor, white-washed walls and black-stained oak beams smothered with bunches of drying herbs.

Three rabbits hung from an old bacon hook near the window.

A long kitchen table took up most of one side of the room; it was covered in rusty agricultural tools and oily parts from some engine or other, presumably a tractor. A couple of tins of rat poison sat at one end, next to a pile of *Picture Post* magazines and a bowl of rotting apples covered in vinegar flies. In one corner of the room stood a television on an upturned diesel drum, and in the other, a mattress covered over with a patchwork quilt, with a bowler hat hanging on a nail above a cracked mirror. A dozen empty Guinness bottles were lined up on the floor beside the mattress. On the wall above, was a signed photograph of a football team called AC Portoferraio, from one of the Italian leagues presumably, though I had never heard of them.

The right side of the room was almost bare. It was dominated by a large, gilt-framed canvas above the fireplace. Even I recognised it: Monica Sahlin's famous painting of her cousin rising to heaven in a wicker-basket, looking wistfully down through a cloud of harebells. On the mantelpiece below stood a sheep's skull with plastic miniature daffodils sprouting from the sockets of the eyes.

On either side of the chimney breast were shelves upon shelves of books and quaintly-bound periodicals, and, in the middle of the room, a small writing desk, with a chair set at an angle as if someone had just got up or was expecting to return. A blank writing pad lay on the desk, and, to one side, a tarnished pewter mug filled with sharpened pencils. On each corner stood a black and white photograph. The one on the left was a very fuzzy snap of a chubby, curly-haired man with a cigarette hanging from his lower lip. My stomach bled sour anxiety, for he looked like my father, who had only once brought me happiness and that was on the day of his dying.

The photo on the right of the desk was of an upright man in a sombre business suit, carrying a furled umbrella. Here, too, was a sense of deja vu: he looked like the men who had chased my mother for the money that my father had borrowed and never repaid. They had harassed me, too, as I was sent to the front door with well-prepared excuses: "Sorry, he's gone to Venezuela on business, and won't be back for six months." I saw again the shock on my grandmother's face when the bailiffs took possession of her house to pay off my father's debts. This was the man who'd told me to send him half of my student grant, and made me feel it was the right thing to do; this was the man who stayed for two years in London hotels without paying his bills, was caught, imprisoned, released on probation and landed a job as general manager of a posh West End hotel, before careering downhill to Butlins. This was the man...

I moved quietly to the centre of the room and almost hit my head against something hanging from one of the beams. It was an old Corona lemonade bottle with a tapered, unstoppered neck. Inside was a little stuffed bird, or so I first thought, but when I looked more closely I was shocked to see it was actually a live wren, sitting on its own droppings, gasping for breath in the thin, warm air that managed to drop down to the bottom. I was trying to work out how the wren had been put in the bottle, when I heard someone spitting. I turned and moved towards the back of the house where a lean-to kitchen and bathroom had been built. I could see a washbasin with a pair of black shoes in it. Next to the basin was a bath, with a man bending so far in that his head was almost touching the bottom. He unfurled and stood upright. I could see something wriggling in his mouth. He turned away and spat into the lavatory bowl. He went back to the bath and leaned over, again stretching down inside. He came back up. There was a large brown spider between his lips.

I back-tracked nervously from the house, and sought refuge in the pub. O'Malley came over.

"Brains?" he asked.

"Look," I said, holding the pump against his pull. He looked up curiously, as the flow stopped and tiny splutters of foam filled the glass. "Small sheds don't have rafters, nothing strong enough to hold a kicking pig."

He put down the glass, and brought across a plate of tapas. "Clams covered in pancetta, then baked."

13

"Shed some light on the mystery."

The awful pun brought a generous smile. "It didn't stay forever with Dai Fern Hill, you know."

"Tell me."

"Geoffrey Faber took it to Tyglyn Aeron."

"Faber? T.S. Eliot's publisher?"

"The very same." He finished pouring my beer, and placed it on the counter with all the satisfaction of a fisherman playing out his line. "Go and see old Eli. I'll give him a ring to say you're coming."

★ ★ ★

I drove to Lampeter to pick up a curry. Lampeter I liked. It was cosmopolitan, just like the part of London we had left. The pasty, chapel-serious faces of the locals were leavened by the black, brown and Chinese faces of students from the college. Hasidim rubbed shoulders with farm labourers in the Spar, hippies strummed in Harford Square, and Muslim women floated down the High Street in deep purdah.

A thickening mist slowed my drive home with the take-away. I remember the table was already laid, and Rachel was in the kitchen making raita, and warming some home-made nan. After that, my memory of what happened is extremely disconnected. We sat down at the table. We lit the candles and said a silent prayer. Rachel was picking up a spoon to serve the rice, and I remember that I was trying to tear the nan bread in two. I heard the creak of the yard gate, and wondered why the geese were so quiet. I heard footsteps outside, someone moving quietly around the yard. Mably was in the back room but, instead of barking furiously as he usually did at the slightest noise, he came whimpering through the house, and flung himself trembling under the table. There was a sound of scuffling feet outside the front door – we have no lobby and the door opens directly into the room where we were eating. I remember looking over my left shoulder, and seeing a white envelope come through the letterbox, and glide down to the doormat. I went across to pick it up. No address on it, just the lines

> *Find meat on bones that soon have none,*
> *And drink in the two milked crags,*
> *The merriest marrow and the dregs*
> *Before the lady's breasts are hags*
> *And the limbs are torn.*

Rachel said something about the food getting cold, so I put the envelope on the table beside me and ate some mutton muglai. Then I saw the envelope move. I stopped eating, picked it up and slit open the back with my knife.

I heard Rachel screaming and the sound of her fork hitting the plate. I jumped to my feet and stood riveted as a black spider came through the slit in the envelope and worked its way towards my hand. The touch of its feet on my finger made me shudder and the envelope fell to the table. Dozens of spiders came spilling out. They scuttled across the table, some abseiling down to the floor, but most running wildly between the plates. Some of the larger ones had already clambered into the silver cartons and were now desperately trying to extricate themselves from the burning curries. I recall seeing three or four small green spiders burrowing into the pilau rice, and Rachel running to the other side of the room.

Foolishly, I picked up a nan and began swotting the spiders but the bread was not well suited to the task. I rushed into the kitchen to fetch a can of fly spray from under the sink. I sprayed it vigorously across the top of the table, Rachel angrily shouting "Poison us, go on, poison us, I would." Then I heard something squealing with pain, the noise a small creature makes when the talons of a hawk strike through its flesh. I dropped the can and ran outside. The orange hazard lights on the car were flashing across the darkening yard. I walked nervously across. I could see the outline of a bird trapped in a layer of mist above the car. A live house martin had been impaled on the aerial.

★ ★ ★

I arrived late at the office the next morning. After a wasted hour shuffling papers across my desk, and wondering about the spiders and the man at Fern Hill, I rang the National Library. Tyglyn Aeron, they said, had been built in the early nineteenth century. Geoffrey Faber had bought it in 1930 and T.S. Eliot was a regular summer guest.

I grabbed a seafood ciabatta from the deli, and drove munching to meet Eli Morgan. O'Malley had said he was a gardener, and that was where I found him, leaning on a spade in the front garden of his small white cottage. He was tall and well-built, and looked surprisingly fit for his age. His eyes were hidden by a peaked cap, so that his face was dominated by the strong chin that jutted out like Mr Punch's, though much broader. We shook hands, and sat on a wooden bench beneath an old apple tree. I clipped a tiny microphone onto his lapel. Old habits die slow. I had carried a tape recorder almost every day of my working life as a sociologist. I could give all my attention to the speaker, not worrying about taking notes or trying to remember what was being said. It would be just as useful in my new role as rural sleuth.

I asked Eli what he remembered about Geoffrey Faber, and let him talk away.

"I worked down there in Tyglyn as second under-gardener, vegetables mostly, which we were sending by train up to London to Faber's house. The Head Gardener was Oaten, who came down here from South Wales with his wife and daughters, and you daren't glance at those girls for Oaten would give you a good beating. He was a brute.

"I seldom was talking to Faber, he was one above us. He was in church sometimes, or the shop. His tongue was sharp if you was upsetting him."

"What did he want with Dai Fern Hill's shed?"

"Somewhere quiet to write, you see."

"For himself, you mean?"

"Eliot."

"Used to write in the shed?"

"That's it."

"Did you ever see Eliot about?"

"He would stay mainly in the house. Sometimes we would see him writing in the shed. He and Faber used to go shooting, I know that. Big bugs they were, they weren't for mixing."

"So Eliot didn't know any locals?"

"Not many."

"None you can remember?"

"Well, that's not for me to say. But there are stories."

We talked a little more about his prize vegetables, and then I left. As I walked down the lane, I had the uneasy feeling that someone was watching me. When I reached the car, I felt that something wasn't quite right, though I couldn't see what. I put the key in the door but it was already unlocked. I looked through the window but could see nothing missing or amiss so I opened the door and climbed in. I turned the ignition and started the engine. I pulled over the seat belt and snapped it in across my chest and looked, as I always did, in the rear view mirror.

But the rear view was missing. Someone had covered the mirror with a piece of paper. There was a verse on it, written in faint red ink:

Chew spider
suck wren
bitch's blood
fountain
penned.
Find meat on bones? Not his.
War on the spider and the wren!

I pulled the paper off, and opened the glove compartment to keep the verse for Rachel. Inside, still oozing blood, was a ring of puppy tails, threaded together with orange baler twine.

I drove fast to the Scadan Coch and asked O'Malley for a glass of RUC, and he quickly poured a double Bushmills into a pint of Guinness. "I've got some tapas for you," I said, putting the tails onto the bar. "Fry for two minutes with sage, onion and tomato and serve in a roll, your original, authentic Ceredigion hot dog, your very own *chien chaud*, serve with relish if not enthusiasm." I quick-marched half the RUC into my stomach. "Look, what the hell's going on?"

"You been asking about the shed?"

"You encouraged me."

"You've upset him somehow." O'Malley lifted the ring of tails from the counter. "I'll fry these over for the ferret."

I finished my drink, and went home, taking the shortcut through the field behind the pub. As I crossed the old bridge, I could see Rachel rounding up the chickens. She was having difficulty in enticing the flighty Seebrights into the coop, and the big Sumatran cockerel was refusing pointblank to go in with the hens. I watched for a minute, enjoying the chaos, and then walked up the dark lane to the cottage.

I let myself in. I was half-way across the room when I saw the upturned bucket on the table. I padded round warily whilst I took off my coat, checked the answering machine and put the kettle on. "It's a letter," said Rachel, coming in with one Seebright still clinging to the top of her shoulder. "I thought it was the safest place to put it."

I rescued the bantam and took it down the garden path to the coop. When I returned, Rachel was standing by the table, fly swat in hand, convinced that the letter contained more wild life. I lifted the bucket, and we stared at the pale lavender envelope. It remained perfectly still but even so Rachel lunged forward and began furiously beating the envelope with her swat.

I picked it up and clipped off a little corner with the kitchen scissors. Nothing came out except the smell of eau-de-cologne. We both relaxed, though Rachel kept the swat in her hand. I slowly slit open the envelope. There was a letter inside, no spiders or puppy tails. I gingerly unfolded the single sheet of paper and read the note out loud: "Come and have coffee this evening. I should like to talk about Mr. Eliot, amongst others. Yours, Rosalind A. Hilton."

★ ★ ★

Rosalind Hilton's welcome was warm and effusive. She insisted on giving me a tour of her cottage, at the same time reeling off the names of the talented people who had lived on the banks of the Aeron. Not just Eliot and Dylan Thomas, she said with pride, but opera singer Sir Geraint Evans at the mouth of the river. "Not to mention," she concluded with a wink, "the new Aeron poets like Rachel Mossman."

"My wife," I said in what I hoped was a modest tone.

"I know," she replied. "I like Rachel's poetry a good deal. She's Jewish, isn't she?"

"Straight out of Hackney."

"And you?"

"No. Her toy goy."

After pouring coffee, Rosalind sat on one side of the fire, and told me to sit opposite. I asked her if I could record our conversation, and after some hesitation, she agreed. Looking across the hearth at her, I guessed she was in her eighties, like old Eli Morgan. Her face was bright and sharp, her hair tied back in a bun. Three gold rings on her right hand gleamed brightly in the light of the fire. She rolled them between the finger and thumb of her other hand, as if she were trying to hypnotise me. Though she looked small and rather frail, when she spoke her voice was so deep and powerful that her presence filled the room.

"I'll come straight to the point, and then, no doubt, you'll want me to start at the beginning." I said that was fine, and then she said in a matter-of-fact voice: "Eliot and I..." She paused and I saw a faint blush on her cheeks, though it might well have been the flames from the fire "...were lovers."

And then she began at the beginning.

"I was born and brought up in the east end of London, in Copley Street, Stepney. My mother's maiden name was Shodken and my father, who was a tailor, was a Hintler. That was a double cross to bear, so to speak, to be Jewish in the 1930s and called Hintler.

"You smile, but it was no joke to be the daughter of Mr and Mrs Hitler, for that was what people called us.

"My parents could see which way things were going in Germany, so in 1935 they made two decisions which they thought would save our lives, or at least make life more tolerable. They changed the family name to Hilton, and we moved out of London to Ciliau Aeron, where I've lived ever since."

"Why Ciliau?"

"Geraint our milkman was always going on about how pretty it was."

"He ran the dairy in Copley Street?"

"Two cows in a tin shed behind the shop, and a churn pulled round the streets on a three-wheeled trolley."

"Did your parents really think that Jews from London could hide in the countryside?"

"Perhaps it was naive but many families did the same. Lubetkin, for instance, who designed the penguin house at London Zoo. He took his family to Gloucestershire, didn't he?"

"But why Wales?"

"It was as far away west as you could get from Europe and the Nazis. And my father had always believed that the Celts were fond of Jews. Perhaps they are, Dylan Thomas certainly was, but I'll come to him in a minute."

"How did you get by?"

"In the time-honoured way. My father did alterations for the bachelor and widowed farmers, my mother took in washing. And we helped out with the haymaking and other farm work. My father was also a scholar – he'd thought seriously of being a Rabbi when he was young but the Communist Party got to him first. The Welsh like scholarship so they took to him quickly.

"No, we told no-one we were Jewish because we were convinced the Germans would eventually invade. We were simply regarded as Londoners who had fled the city for a quiet country life. We were treated politely and kindly, if a little suspiciously. Within a month of being here, my parents were going to church. It caused them some pain but not much. They were both atheists and hadn't been religious Jews since their early teens. Going to church was part of the new identity, like going to the agricultural shows and the *eisteddfodau*. The worst thing was getting rid of our duvets – *deks*, we called them – and learning to sleep with blankets. Only Jews had duvets at that time, and my parents didn't want to keep anything that would give us away."

"Didn't you miss London?"

"Strangely enough, no. I already knew that I had a little talent for painting and that blossomed here in the countryside. I loved the sea, which I had only ever seen once or twice before. I could wear lipstick without being hissed at by the neighbours, some of whom were very *frum*. Here we had our own little cottage, but in Copley Street we all lived upstairs in three rooms, with Mrs Presse and her children downstairs. The lavatory was at the bottom of the garden, and we had to go through Mrs Presse's kitchen to reach it. I didn't miss that, I can tell you, and besides, I felt at home here."

"Really?"

"Wales is Old Testament country – the men were Isaac and Jacob and Esau, and the villages Carmel, Hebron and Bethlehem, even a Sodom or two. You see, Wales is Palestine, Syria and Mesopotamia rolled up into one. It was *heimisher*.

"Social life? I had little of that in London. I was more interested in books and painting, and, besides, not many wanted to date the daughter of Mr Hitler. Down here it was better. I went on rambles with the theology students from Lampeter, and that helped both my painting and my Welsh. And on Friday evenings there was always a dance in Aberaeron. I used to catch the train in with the two Oaten girls and we had a wonderful time.

"Within a year of arriving, I was helping out at Tyglyn when the Fabers were down. I was just a general handy girl. Sometimes I looked after the children when the nanny was ill. If there were guests for dinner, I helped in the kitchen or prepared the tables for auction bridge. And that is how I first met Eliot. I was sitting on a bench in the garden sketching. Eliot came out of his shed and walked down the path towards me. He stood behind me for a while, watching as I sketched. Then he sat down. I noticed how fastidiously he arranged his plus fours, which he always wore at Tyglyn. He sat with me for about twenty minutes. We talked mainly of painting and he wanted to know what I thought of the Surrealists. I knew nothing of them, I'm afraid, and he gave me a little lecture on Salvador Dali. That was to be the first of many conversations. And the next year, I met Dylan Thomas. Such things could not have happened to me in Stepney.

"I'll tell you a bit about Dylan and then go back to Eliot. It was in July 1936, in the evening. I was alone in Tyglyn baby-sitting – I think the nanny had been got rid of by then. The Fabers were at a poetry reading at another mansion just up the road. Eliot was upstairs in his room writing. There was a hammering on the door. I opened it and this young man with tousled hair stood there, looking slightly unkempt in corduroy trousers and a black polo-neck sweater. I noticed a two-seater sports car in the drive with an older man with flaming red hair behind the driving wheel. The young man came into the hall, looked about and said: "Where's Vernon hiding?" I replied that he had come to the wrong house, and that if he wished to hear Mr Watkins read then I could re-direct him.

"He gave me a huge smile and said he'd much prefer to read some poetry to me. He stretched out his hand and said 'I'm Dylan Thomas.' Well, of course I'd heard of him. Eliot had mentioned him. And my father was always talking about him, too.

"I invited him into the Drawing Room, and he fell back into the red leather sofa and almost disappeared between the cushions, he was quite slim, really, at least he was then. I asked him if he'd like a drink and he said yes, but nothing alcoholic. I had the impression that he was recovering from an illness and he'd been told to stay off alcohol for a while."

"I suppose he wanted sweets," I said.

"No, he asked for a glass of milk and cake, so I went to the kitchen and brought some for him. There was a certain chemistry between us straight away. After all, I was twenty-one at the time and he was only a year older. I told him that Eliot was writing upstairs and asked if he would like to meet him. 'What, and play altar boy to his Pope?'

"He stayed for more than an hour. He asked to see the Library, and he sniffed along the shelves like a truffle hound. He found some Hardy, which he read to me, and then Rilke, *das Stündenbuch,* I think, which I read to him, translating as I went along. Then a quick tour of the house, avoiding upstairs. We talked a lot about London, and he asked me about Copley Street and all the goings-on. He said he was fascinated by neighbours because his father hated them so much. He soon picked up it was a mainly Jewish street, so I told him, rather cleverly I thought, that we used to give our Jewish neighbours a box of Matzos at Passover, and they would give us a pudding at Christmas.

"Copley Street felt like thin ice so I changed the subject and told him about the Faber's home-made electricity. There was a waterwheel in the farmyard linked to a generator, which fed into a very large bank of lead accumulators in a room next to the kitchen. He wanted to see it for himself, and that's how we spent the time. And, of course, to the kitchen for more milk and some widgeon pie that had been left out for Eliot's supper. Dylan ate it all. On the way out, he took Eliot's scarf, only for a borrow, he said, but he never returned it. He asked me to help him put on his jumper, which I did, though I thought it rather odd. And off he went to find Vernon."

★   ★   ★

I felt buoyant and pleased with myself. It had been a good interview, and Rosalind Hilton had asked me to come back to talk some more. Maybe I should have gone straight home but I didn't, and in retrospect that may have been a mistake. I drove, without really thinking much about it, to Fern Hill. Perhaps I was taking myself too seriously, but I wanted to know why we were being sent unsolicited spiders and puppy tails.

It took only a few minutes to get there. I parked the car, and got the torch from the boot. Not that there was much use for it because the moon was full and shining brightly. I padded cautiously up to the farmhouse. I stopped at the edge of the yard. I could hear owls, and no doubt they were watching me as I watched the house. Something was whimpering in the barn but I couldn't make out what it was. The vinegar scent of burning oak disinfected the air, which stank of rotting flesh, perhaps a sheep somewhere in the trees at the back of the house.

One of the downstairs windows was lit up, and cast a yellow light onto the cobbles of the yard. I moved slowly and quietly forwards. I could see him in the square of the window, as if I had chanced upon a portrait in a secluded part of a gallery. He was crouched over the desk, his chin cupped in both hands. His two index fingers were behind his ear lobes which he pushed absent-mindedly back and forth. He was looking at a notebook in front of him, and once or twice he would take a pencil from the pot, try to write something, and then put it back again. As he did this, he would glance at one of the photographs on the desk, and then at the other, shaking his head as he did so.

I found myself thinking of paintings I knew but I couldn't quite conjure them up. A Rembrandt, perhaps, a man huddled over a kitchen table...Van Gogh looking at his face in the mirror...and then, without warning, I was taken over by a vision of myself sitting at a table. I wasn't outside the farmhouse at all, I was inside another room, in another house. In front of me was a plate, with four fat sausages on it, at which I picked with my fork. I heard a great whooshing noise behind me. I looked round just as the fishing rod peeled into my back.

"Eat those sausages," thundered my father.

I jumped to my feet in shock. "I hate fat sausages," I cried out.

"They're just the same as thin ones."

"In that case, why can't I have thin ones?" I retorted, and this time the rod came down across the side of my face.

I felt angry but also disappointed. I rushed forward and hit him. He fell back into the armchair, sprawled like a boxer on his stool, waiting for the trainer's sponge. Blood spurted from his nose and drenched the front of the white shirt that I had ironed for him before going to school.

He stood up from the chair...and I was outside the farmhouse window again. I saw him cross the room, and heard the door open. I crouched so low that I could feel the cool of the ground on my face. He stood in the doorway looking across the yard, sniffed the air several times, and then fumbled with his trouser zip.

"Do not come, gentile, into my good night," he whispered. A stream of water splashed onto the cobbles with such force that it sprayed sideways across my hands and face. He went back inside and bolted the door.

I ran across the farm yard and back to the car. I remember nothing of the journey home. There was a fine smell in the house as I came through the front door, and Rachel called from the kitchen: "Ready to eat?"

"What you got?" I asked, making my way to the bathroom to wash away the stink of urine.

"Red cabbage."

"And?"

"Sauté potatoes."

"And?"

"Bratwurst."

★ ★ ★

The next morning I drove to Rosalind Hilton's, and took some home-made bagels with me. I know how to get on with the natives. She found some smoked sewin and cream cheese, put them on the coffee table between us, and was ready to talk.

"People think that Eliot and Thomas were chalk and cheese. Well, to some extent they're right. Eliot liked order and discipline around him, Dylan lived in chaos and dirt. Eliot was cool, reserved, the great chiller, you might think, but Dylan was warm, out-going, in public at least."

"Eliot the Harvard graduate..."

"And Dylan, the failure at grammar school..."

"The banker and the scrounger, the cat lover and the cat hater..."

"Dylan had an absolute craving for sweets. Eliot sneered at them. Pointless self-gratification, he said. That rather sums them up, I think," said Rosalind tartly.

"Did they have anything in common?"

"Oh, yes, love of the sea for one thing, and molly-coddling mothers, for another."

"They were both frail children," I said, as if Rosalind needed an explanation. "And sickly for most of their lives."

"Isn't it curious that they both married in secret and to women obsessed with dancing?"

"I understand Dylan and Eliot were rather puritanical about sex..."

"...and neither was very good at it," interrupted Rosalind.

I wanted to ask how she knew but I was a little taken aback by her frankness. I decided to leave it for later. I could see that Rosalind was impatient to continue.

"Drinking was important to both of them," she said, "but other things, too. Dylan loved his bed, sucking a beer bottle, eating cake, reading trash novels. Eliot had his detective stories, and was totally obsessed with murders altogether."

"And politics?"

"Dylan was never political, except when it suited him, but he found Eliot's right-wing views distasteful. He was very upset when he heard about Eliot's tirade against the Jews. Eliot had given a lecture somewhere, and talked about America being invaded by foreign races. I knew nothing about Eliot's anti-semitism until much later, and saw no signs of it myself.

"I'll say one more thing about Eliot and the Jews: he may have thought a society should be based on blood-kinship, as he put it, but he certainly didn't put that concept into practice himself – not when his trousers were down, anyway.

"Well, that brings us nicely to sex. My parents, you understand, were communists and free thinkers. They passed to me no hang ups about sex or related matters. From my early years, I was always encouraged to think for myself, and to care little for convention."

Rosalind paused. I wasn't clear whether she was having difficulty in recalling events or whether she was looking for courage to continue.

"My first full sexual encounter was with a Baptist student called Mansel, whilst we were on a painting excursion in Snowdonia. It was a chilly experience. Thereafter, there were a number of men, mainly students, or others interested in the arts. We saw ourselves as part of the bohemian rainbow, and this sharing of our bodies was perfectly natural. I want you to know this because I would want no-one to believe that, when I went to London to visit Dylan, I was a sweet and innocent country girl who was cruelly exploited by a rapacious poet. On the contrary. As I remember things, it was I who did the taking to bed, and when I got him there, I found that I was more experienced, or at least adept, in these matters than was he."

"When was this?"

"Early in 1938. After that, we met once or twice a year, and then quite frequently when he moved to Talsarn."

"And Eliot? How did that begin?"

"We became good friends on his visits to Tyglyn. I was always in and out of the Faber house. He liked to walk with me along the river, and he would write whilst I sketched. He would always take his binoculars in case we came across an interesting bird. My father was a twitcher too, and Eliot helped him log the kites. They got on quite well, and Eliot loved talking in our front room with Dad.

"They argued a lot about Germany and what was happening in Europe. I remember vividly one occasion in 1940. They had talked all afternoon. They came out of the front room after tea. My father took Eliot to the door. Both looked flustered and overwrought and shook hands rather stiffly. Eliot walked down the path without looking back. My father shouted after him: 'Mr Eliot, why do you and Mr Pound sneer at us so?' It was as if the world had ended. All those church services and *eisteddfodau* for nothing!

"When Eliot came down the next year, I sensed there was something different about him. He certainly seemed more approachable, less guarded. I was a little frosty after what had happened the previous year, but I found, to my dismay, that I also wanted to ingratiate myself...I think I must have felt our future was in his hands."

"How was he different?"

"He seemed more inclined to touch me, which was extremely unusual for Eliot. He would take my elbow over a stile, tap me on the shoulder to draw my attention. That definitely hadn't happened before. One day we went out along the Beech Walk and turned up the hill. It's quite a steep climb, and when you get there you can see the sea. We were about half way up when I lost my footing and slipped. Eliot put out his arm and caught me round the waist. His hand stayed there until we reached the top. I turned to thank him, and kissed him on the cheek. He held my hands and said: 'This is our last summer together. They're selling the estate.'

"The next day he asked me to go to New Quay Fair with him, and Oaten drove us over. We walked around the booths, and I put my arm through his, though he took no interest in me or the booths, and seemed to be searching for something else. It turned out to be the boxing ring. Well, actually it was nothing of the sort, just a patch of grass squared off with rope and fence posts. We stayed there most of the afternoon. Some big bruiser from Bristol was taking on the local farm lads. Eliot was fascinated, he screamed and shouted for all he was worth. The man from Bristol made short work of most of the lads. Except one.

"I felt someone pushing their way through the crowd from the back, and the people making way for him, almost respectfully. He was quite young, stocky like a prop forward, huge hands. And he was black. That really shocked Eliot, I could see.

"He was well known to the locals, for they cheered and cheered when he climbed in the ring. He took off his shirt, and laid it carefully in one corner. He took out a small tin from his pocket and rubbed his body with grease till his chest gleamed like cocoa in candle-light. The man from Bristol was taunting him, I can't remember what he said, but nowadays we would say it was racist. The young man took no notice, and calmly came to the centre of the ring.

"The referee started the fight and then quickly jumped out of the way. The two men moved around each other cautiously. A few blows were landed, but not many, and then a handbell was rung to end the round. As the young boy turned to go back to his corner, the Bristol man hit him on the side of the head. Well, that made the crowd absolutely livid and for a moment we thought they'd invade the ring and lynch him.

"The second round was pretty bloody, and I can only say that Eliot was engrossed. I doubt if he knew I was beside him, or that half of west Wales were shouting their heads off behind us. It lasted far longer than it should have, because someone forgot to ring the bell, or if they did, no-one heard it. Eventually, the local policeman climbed into the ring and dragged the two men apart.

"As the third round started, someone shouted some comment about the Bristol man's legs. The crowd burst out laughing. The young boy lost his concentration, and was hit badly. He staggered back across the ring and fell on the grass. The crowd went silent again. Eliot whooped with joy and gave me a hug. He leaned forward and kissed me. You might describe it as passionate.

"The young boy staggered to his feet, and they threw a bucket of cold water over him. He came forward, quite steady and snarling. He threw one punch to the Bristol man's face, squashing his nose and mouth, and he collapsed. The crowd cheered wildly and some started singing 'Bread of Heaven'. He was up on eight, and staggered back to the ropes. The young boy moved in, and that was it. The Bristol man pretended to stumble, the boy hesitated and was caught on the side of his face. His legs gave way, and he dropped to the grass. And there was Eliot, leaping to his feet, arms outstretched in joy, suddenly twisting in mid-air as if he were a dog catching a fly. Then he dropped to the ground, and was scrabbling round on his hands and knees, looking for something in the grass. He jumped up with this wonderful smile on his face and held out his upturned hand. It was a blood-smeared tooth, lying there like a beached seal pup. He unscrewed the top of his cane, put the tooth in the top, and screwed it back on again. He took me in his arms, and kissed me again.

"We caught the little bus back to Ciliau, though I felt like making my own way home. The incident with the tooth had upset me. We sat in the front seat and Eliot talked, rather incoherently as if he were drunk, about the time he had spent in Paris. It was early evening when we arrived back at the house. The Fabers were out. Eliot rang the bell in the drawing room and asked Annie to prepare some food. He paced about, still muttering about Paris, and took two or three sizeable whiskies. After we'd eaten, we walked down to the river, and came back up the field to the Beech Walk. By now, we were holding hands. We stopped at the walled garden, and went down the path to his shed. He shuffled his papers about, had another whisky from a bottle that was hidden in a bag of compost, and said something silly about not being able to get a decent bottle of Irish whiskey so the next best thing was to put the scotch in peat.

"I took his hands, pulled him towards me and put his head on my shoulder. I put one hand on the back of his neck and the other around his waist. He went completely limp and folded into me. I stroked the back of his head and he started to moan. 'Tom,' I said in my best encouraging voice, 'please kiss me.' And he came to life...it was as if I had just pulled the plug on the Hoover dam. There was another passionate kiss, and he started fumbling with the buttons of my cardigan. And then disaster! An uproar in the garden. We could hear someone running down the path. Eliot leapt away from me and sat down at his little desk. I took up a studied pose at the window, looking down across the river. Oaten burst in, and was clearly disappointed to see that it was only Eliot and me in the shed. 'There's bloody poachers hiding about,' he cried and went off down the garden.

"Anyway, it was all shattered by Oaten's interruption. We

walked back up to the house and I wondered how I might ever again pull Eliot back into some semblance of ordinary humanity. I needn't have worried because he was plotting his own escape. Annie brought us some coffee. Eliot diligently laid out the cups and poured the coffee and milk. He passed the cup to me, and I asked for some sugar. He had some ready on a spoon. He dropped it in the cup and immediately the coffee started to fizz, and scores of little fish popped up on the surface. Eliot was in hysterics. I was annoyed, it seemed such a childish thing to do. He came over, lifted me from the chair, and said: 'I've only ever known dull duty.'

"We embraced, and he whispered: 'My sweetest Volupine.' We went upstairs to his room. There wasn't much in the way of preliminaries, not least because the room was so chilly. Eliot was hesitant at first, and there was a spot of embarrassment over his truss, which he didn't really want me to see. Anyway, I'll spare you the details. Sophisticated he was not, but he was certainly lustful. We were at it all night, playing Bola, as he called it. A few weeks later, I realised that I was pregnant."

"And Eliot was the father?"

"Or Dylan." She paused, and looked away into the fire. "Dylan came to see me the following week."

"Did you tell them?"

"Dylan seemed rather taken aback, if not a little shocked. But we went for a long walk along the Aeron and by the time we'd come back, he was more like his usual self, and quite excited at the thought of another son, as he assumed it would be.

"Eliot was different. He seemed pleased at first, but when I told him I couldn't be sure that he was the father, that it might as easily be Dylan, he was furious. No, not with me, but with Dylan, for some reason. He wasn't at all rational about it and went off in a rage."

"And what happened?"

"I stayed good friends with them both. Dylan would drive across to see us once or twice a year. I saw a lot of him when they were in New Quay, at Majoda."

"And Eliot...?"

"He came less frequently, but wrote quite a lot."

"And the child...?"

"A boy, born the same week as Aeronwy, but a year older. That was always a problem for Dylan, two birthdays in the same week. I felt sorry for Caitlin, he wasn't with her when Aeronwy was born, and she assumed he'd been pubbing. This was the time when she realised that Dylan had become two people, as she put it, though she didn't know the reason. Anyway, he did his best for her. He left here soon after Waldo's first birthday party, and rushed up to London in my father's old dressing gown. It was terribly cold and that's all I could find in the house for him, but he was too late for Aeronwy's birth."

"And that was his name? Waldo."

"Waldo Sweeney Hilton. I asked each of them to choose a name for him, and that's what they picked."

"What did he like to be called?"

"Oh, definitely Waldo."

I wondered if appearance would provide any clues so I asked her who he looked like.

"He has Eliot's height and build, but it's Dylan's nose he's got."

"Does he know about them?"

"They were uncles to begin with, but I told him the day that Dylan died, the whole truth."

"How did he take it?"

"Very badly. I'm sure it's why he failed the scholarship. He became very introspective. And he really missed Dylan. He didn't visit very often, but when he did he made such a fuss of Waldo, especially on his birthday. Dylan loved birthdays, and he only once missed one of Waldo's.

"Mind you, he lost interest when Waldo started growing up. He only liked them when they were babies. By the way, have you noticed there are no proper families in *Milk Wood*, except Butcher Beynon's?"

"I'm not sure what you mean."

"There aren't any children in Llareggub."

"Polly Garter's?"

"That's my point. There's only her babies, and Lily Smalls, the teenager. There's nothing in between. True, there are children in the school playground, but never with their families. It has something to do with the way Dylan was excluded by his own father. Do you and Rachel have any children?"

"No."

"Never wanted any?"

This was not something I wished to discuss, and it was taking me away from the interview.

"What happened to Waldo?"

"You could try asking him yourself."

"He lives here?"

"No, at Fern Hill."

★ ★ ★

We paused for lunch. I walked around outside, whilst Rosalind prepared the food, and I wondered how such a person could be the mother of someone who eats spiders, and makes presents of puppy tails. I was rather absent-mindedly admiring the cottage, when I noticed a note under the windscreen wiper of my car. I was in no doubt who'd left it there. I went out of the wicker gate onto the road, and pulled the paper from under the wiper. It simply said

> Rat's hair, dogskin, owlheart,
> Pigs' eyes, womanchop.
> Stir well and stew the lot.

I went back inside. There were curried turkey sandwiches, and a herb and rabbit pâté which, Rosalind said with pride, Waldo had prepared. I took the sandwiches. We drank from a pitcher of wine that Rosalind had made herself from vine leaves and sage. It was slightly medicinal, like a weak Campari, but it cut cleanly through the rich tastes of the sandwiches. I wanted to know more about Eliot, and asked her to tell me what happened after Dylan's death.

"Eliot took a lot more interest, but that caused quite a few problems. He wanted to take Waldo out of the secondary modern and pay for him to go to public school. That started a major row. He also objected to Waldo's not going to church. But on the plus side, he set up a trust fund for him in New York."

"Eliot was taking his responsibilities seriously?"

"Partly, but he was also buying his way in, and that was fine by me. I wanted Waldo provided for."

"What did Eliot want in exchange?"

"His Princess Volupine."

"Did he get her?"

"Yes, he got his princess, his Jewish princess."

"The typist in 'The Waste Land'."

"There was no other way, Martin. I was past the haymaking age, and was no good at sewing farmers' fly buttons back on, or raising their turn-ups."

"Did you ever tell Waldo he was Jewish?"

"He found out quite by accident. We were clearing out the house, just after my father had died. There was an old trunk in the small bedroom. We opened it together, Waldo had to lever the lid off with a crow bar. And what did we find sitting on top? A skull cap! And a *menorah*. I was so angry with them. All that pretence to hide from the Germans..."

I hesitated for a minute, and then plunged straight in. "You know he's sending me funny letters?" I passed the latest note across for her to read.

"He's only doing what he's been told."

"By you?"

She looked up angrily. "Of course not." After a moment's silence, she said: "Waldo's not well, you know."

That I did know.

"I'm sorry, I should have explained sooner." She was twisting the ring on her finger so violently that I could see a small bruise appearing. "He hears voices."

"Any old voices?" I asked, sounding more flippant than I'd intended.

"Voices from his father's pen."

"Which father?"

"Dylan."

"The voices from *Milk Wood*?" I asked, this time sounding incredulous.

"Usually Beynon the butcher."

Beynon the hunter of wild giblets. Sneaking up on corgis with his cleaver, swaggering down Coronation Street with a finger in his mouth, not his own, purveyor of the finest shrew and budgie rissoles...

"Waldo's always been fascinated by Mr Beynon."

Fox pâté, cats' liver, mole surprise and otter pie...

"I hope Waldo's letters haven't upset Rachel."

Heart of owl, eye of mouse, tail of puppy-dog...

"Waldo's quite harmless really."

Slice of buttock, cut of thigh, womanchop...

I rushed from the cottage and drove recklessly fast through the narrow lanes. I found our back door open and no sign of Rachel. I searched the outbuildings, the garden and the hut where she sometimes wrote her poetry. Then I remembered that she often went with Mably at this time of day to walk by the river. I ran down the hill, crossed the old bridge and crashed wildly through the trees to the river bank. I followed the path past the walled garden, and as I rounded the corner near the otter pool, I saw Rachel leaning against the wall with Mably lying on the ground beside her. I hugged her until it hurt and she squealed in protest.

"I'm glad you're all right."

"I'm fine but the dog isn't. He won't move."

Mably looked panic stricken, the look he always had at the vet's. "What scared him?"

"We came around the corner and saw a man standing by the hide. Mably rushed up to him barking like he always does. The man touched him on the head and Mably fell to the ground. By the time I got there, the man had disappeared."

We pulled, shoved and cajoled Mably but eventually we had to pick him up and carry him home. He lay in his basket for the rest of the afternoon, and not even food would entice him out. The vet came and pronounced him fit and well. We had supper, watched television and went to bed. I came down in the morning to make tea, and Mably was dead in his basket.

* * *

It was not easy going back to Rosalind Hilton's, but it was helped by knowing that Rachel would be safe, out all day at Welsh classes. We had buried Mably by the poetry hut, near a spot we knew would be covered in daffodils in the spring. We had stood silently whilst the Aeron rushed past, and then trudged tearfully back to the house. I left Rachel at the bus stop, and drove to Rosalind's, pondering on how recent events had affected our relationship – it seemed that her son had killed our dog, and perhaps our own well-being was at stake. I felt responsible for what had happened, but I also wanted to see things through to a settled outcome. It wasn't in my nature to let matters hang in the air, incomplete. And, to be honest, I felt excited at the prospect of unravelling the mystery that was being spun in front of me. I'd been engaged to find a missing shed that was linked to both Dylan Thomas and T.S. Eliot, but it was giving me the opportunity to investigate, through Rosalind's story, their lives and works. Sleuth and sociologist were coming together in one project, and that was very satisfying.

Besides, where was the proof that the man Rachel had encountered was Waldo Hilton? I resolved to say nothing at the moment, and I arrived just as Rosalind was making coffee. We sat as usual next to the fire, and I switched the tape to record.

"There was the most awful row one year. I think it was early 1944, and Waldo was just coming up to his second birthday. Eliot was lecturing in Swansea and when he'd finished he came to stay for a few days. I was still quite fond of him then. He used to spend the morning writing, and then after lunch we would catch the bus to New Quay and walk along the beach. We had just returned from one of those walks when I heard a car pull up. I looked out and it was Dylan, jumping out of a taxi.

"I opened the door and went down the path to meet him. I thought it was better that Eliot saw as little as possible of Dylan's greeting, because he was usually exceptionally affectionate, and often a little lewd. I was carrying Waldo and, thank goodness, that helped to cramp Dylan's style a little. As we entered the house, Dylan stopped and sniffed the air. 'Cats,' he said, 'the bloody place stinks of cats.' It wasn't that he didn't like cats, they just closed his chest up, as if he were asthmatic. Then he saw Eliot and said: 'Dr Crippen, I presume?'

"Eliot nodded his head and said: 'Good afternoon, Mr. Thomas.'

"Dylan hated that kind of affected politeness, and, sure enough, he farted. Loudly. Then he held Waldo up in the air, the way most men seem to want to do with babies, and said: 'And how's my little flannel-bottom.'

'*Yours*, Mr Thomas?' said Eliot, reaching out to take Waldo from Dylan.

'Bugger off.'

'Fine words from a man who pretends to be a poet.'

'*Pretends*, Mr Eliot, *pretends*?'

'Such coarseness sits uneasily with responsible fatherhood, Mr Thomas.'

'You know as much about fatherhood, Mr Eliot, as I know about banking,' replied Dylan, which was true in a way because Eliot had had no children in his own marriage. By this time, I had prised Waldo away from Dylan and put him down in his cot. It was just as well. Eliot crossed the room, and shoved Dylan out through the door. He tried to close it but Dylan managed to wedge it open with his foot. They were both shouting at each other, the baby had started to cry and I was in tears. I grabbed Eliot and dragged him away from the door. Dylan burst through, and threw a punch that skidded off Eliot's shoulder. Eliot didn't respond but stood there smiling down rather condescendingly at

Dylan. I managed to get between them and Dylan backed off. Eliot continued to sneer and Dylan said: 'Don't play the church warden with me, you trussed-up prig.'

"Now I swear Dylan knew nothing about Eliot's truss. How could he? I certainly hadn't told him, any more than I had told Eliot that Dylan rarely wore underpants. It was just a chance remark. Eliot went incandescent, I knew how sensitive he was about the truss, and how wounded he must have felt.

"Eliot left the room and came back carrying his suitcase. 'You're welcome to stay, Mr. Thomas, but remember, I shall do everything in my power to keep the boy. Everything.'

"Dylan turned to me: 'Let the old fart go. It's time you had a young man singing in your sheets.'

"The rest of the year was fairly uneventful. Eliot sent me a series of letters asking me to make him Waldo's legal guardian but I refused. He suggested we came to live in London. It was not difficult to say 'no' to that. There were more letters from his solicitors but I ignored them, too. And, fair play, he always sent presents down to Waldo, including, of course, lots of practical jokes which were of no use at all to a baby. Still, at least he was thinking about Waldo, and that meant something to me.

"In September, Dylan moved into Majoda bungalow, just outside New Quay. He was happy living there, always boasting about the wonderful views he had of the bay, with a pub just down the road for the evenings."

"What was Majoda like to live in?"

"The rooms were tiny and the walls were thin. There was nowhere quiet for Dylan to write. So I arranged for Eliot's shed from Tyglyn Aeron to be taken down and put on the cliff next to the bungalow. That made Dylan very happy though I didn't dare tell him that Eliot had used it for writing.

"October started badly. Vernon Watkins and Gwen were getting married, and Dylan was to be the best man. He was very excited about it, and asked me to come up to London, and Waldo, of course. The worst of the blitz was over, I'd been away for almost ten years and the thought of going back was too much to resist. We travelled up in a train crowded with troops, but I was never without a seat. The plan was that Dylan would attend the wedding, whilst Waldo and I would go down to Stepney, and maybe find some of our old neighbours there.

"We were on our way to drop me off, with plenty of time to spare for Dylan to get to the church, when Waldo had a seizure. This was the very first sign of something seriously wrong with him. It was the most frightening moment of my life, but thank God we were in London where there were plenty of hospitals. Dylan ordered the driver to take us to St. Mary's which he thought the nearest, though he was wrong about that. Directions weren't his strength, and he ignored the driver who said there was one much closer. Anyway, we were at St. Mary's all afternoon. Waldo settled down, but they wanted to keep him in for observation. I was distraught and Dylan refused to leave me. He had missed the wedding but he could still have gone to the reception. 'Vernon will understand,' he said, and we both stayed near the hospital overnight.

"Vernon was devastated, Gwen was furious and all Dylan's biographers have been beastly about it since. Of course, he was never able to tell Vernon what had really happened because no-one, not even Vernon, knew about me and Waldo, and nor would they ever.

"After Waldo's seizure, Dylan spend a fortune on doctors. He wanted the best, and remember there wasn't much of a health service then. When he went to Prague, they told him about a special clinic for children like Waldo. Dylan paid for us to go there for three months. It must have cost a fortune, though it didn't help very much.

"You can see now why Dylan was always on the cadge. Even after the war, when he was earning quite well, he was always borrowing from his friends. Caitlin could never understand why he had so little money to spare.

"Christmas came and went, Dylan arrived on New Year's Day looking the worse for wear, and he spent most of the time in the rocker near the Aga, drinking milk and feeding himself and

Waldo with the leftover plum pudding. In the evening, we sat in the parlour in front of a roaring fire. I was reading a book and Dylan was bouncing Waldo up and down on his knees. I remember Dylan saying: 'What's Christmas without an uncle?' when a huge piece of coal fell out of the grate and rolled across the hearth onto some newspapers that we'd foolishly left on the carpet. They caught fire instantly. Dylan put Waldo in the cot, and rushed to the kitchen to fetch water. But the pipes were frozen. I started to stamp on the papers as best I could but without making much of an impression. Next thing, Dylan was racing back and forth with armfuls of snow and dumping them on the flames, looking for all the world like someone carrying a baby in swaddling clothes. I believe it was that piece of coal that started Dylan off on *A Child's Christmas*.

"Things began to go sour in the New Year, particularly with the shooting. You know the story?"

I nodded. It had been the most sensational event of Dylan's life. He'd escaped death by inches. There'd been a quarrel in the Black Lion in New Quay with a war-weary special forces commando called William Killick. After a brief exchange of blows, Killick had been thrown out of the pub by Alastair Graham, an old friend of Dylan's. Graham was extremely well connected, with friends in government and the royal family. He had come to live in New Quay after resigning from the diplomatic service. His bacchanalian house parties were a gay assortment of London friends, so much so that his mansion became known locally as Bugger Hall.

"Graham drove Dylan home to Majoda. We were playing some silly games when the shooting began. Then Killick burst in, and threatened to blow us all up."

"But no-one was hurt?"

"No. Dylan was on his knees licking Caitlin's legs pretending to be her spaniel, and the rest of us were on the floor drinking beer out of cereal bowls – it was Dylan's favourite party game. The bullets went right overhead, thank God.

"Dylan was marvellous. He was the bravest of the lot, and

took the gun away from Killick. And then he worked out the cover story for everybody. That's how Dylan became involved with British intelligence. Alastair was very impressed and arranged for Dylan to meet Ian Fleming."

"As in James Bond?"

"Yes, though he hadn't written anything at that point. He was high up in naval intelligence, I believe. Anyway, Dylan played along, it was great fun for him, but he was flattered, too, and he needed the money. He went to lunch at All Souls, with Rouse I think, and that's where the deal was done, in the rose garden, early 1946."

"I just can't see Dylan as a spy."

"Intelligence was full of writers in those days – it was excellent cover."

"What did they ask him to do?"

"They used him in the BBC at first, keeping an eye on the lefties. They were worried about a communist ring there. They sent him to Italy in 1947, and then to Prague, just sniffing around the intellectuals, and reporting back, pockets of resistance, underground press, civil liberties, that sort of thing.

"No, he wasn't strictly on the payroll, just cash in hand for each job and a small retainer. They used Margaret Taylor to channel the money to him. And it was MI6 who paid for the Boat House."

"And the trip to Iran for the oil company?"

"Now that was rather interesting. One of MI6's agents in Iran had sent a message claiming he had a list of Soviet spies who had infiltrated British intelligence and the Foreign Office. His difficulty was, of course, that he didn't know who to trust with this information, so he insisted that they sent out someone known to him, and he suggested Dylan. MI6 knew that the oil company had plans to make a film, so it was just a question of making sure that Dylan was given the job of scriptwriter."

"But why Dylan?"

"The agent in Iran was Araf Lloyd-Morgan. His father was an engineer from Laugharne, and his mother a local girl working in the accounts department. The company put him through school, he was very bright, and they saw quickly what an asset he would be to them. Araf went to the university in Tehran and then the company sent him to Oxford for a year, and that's where he met Dylan, and became good friends. But MI6 had spotted Araf's potential, too, and they recruited him."

"So Dylan agreed to go and collect Araf's list?"

"Not at first. He simply refused. His marriage was in tatters, because Caitlin had learnt of his affairs in America. And he didn't relish the prospect of six weeks in the desert with nobody but oil men for company. But MI6 leaned on him, blackmail really. They had John Davenport intercept the love letters that had been sent to Dylan at his club."

"I thought Margaret Taylor had done that."

"Did you ever think how a woman could enter a men's club and get hold of a member's letters? No, it was Davenport. So they told Dylan that they'd send one of the love letters each week to Caitlin until he agreed to go to Iran. Of course, he caved in, and he went out to make the film. Araf passed on his list to Dylan to bring home. And that's where it all went wrong.

"Dylan was supposed to take the list to Harold Nicolson, who would pass it to the Cabinet Secretary. But as soon as Dylan set foot in London, he went on the binge. He ended up in the Gargoyle with the usual cronies. Guy Burgess was there – he and Dylan had been great friends for a long time. He gave Araf's envelope to Burgess: 'Give this to Old Nick – save me going into the office tomorrow.' Dylan was anxious to get back to Laugharne to repair things with Caitlin, and he caught the milk train that night.

"Burgess, of course, opened the envelope, and found his name on the list. Three days later, Araf was killed in a car crash in Tehran, not an accident, Philby's doing. It gave Burgess enough time to warn the others, and in June he defected to the Soviets, and the others went soon after."

"It was Dylan's fault they all got away?"

"Oh yes. And they took everything with them. Nuclear secrets, lists of our agents, defence deployments, the lot."

"You're saying that Dylan's mistake helped the Russians catch up in the arms race?"

"Yes, the final irony. He hated those bombs so much. He was devastated. Didn't write a line of poetry after that."

"And no more work for intelligence?"

"Of course not. And in the end, they had to get rid of him. He'd worked out what the Americans were up to in Iran in 1953, and didn't like it. The CIA intercepted his letters to Bert Trick. The last straw was his suing *Time* magazine. They couldn't risk anything coming out. So the Agency leaned on the hospital."

"You mean..?"

"A winking injection too far."

"That's unbelievable!"

"It was the height of the Cold War. No chances were taken."

★　★　★

I left Rosalind's, drove home the back way, and called in to see O'Malley. The pub was packed and I could smell why. There were plates of roulade on the tables, most likely spinach or chard, chopped garlic sausages, and slices of fried aubergine. O'Malley came across, with a Brains in one hand, and a small plate of sausages and roulade in the other. "You know something," I said to him as I picked up the beer, "when my mother was alive, we always had thin sausages."

She and my father ran an oil and hardware business. We had a shop on the main street of the village, and a green Commer van that toured the farms and council estates. Selling paraffin had been in the family for three generations. The business declined under my father's stewardship and eventually he was declared a bankrupt. This was largely because of his liking for long holidays in expensive hotels (where he called himself Wing Commander, though he had never been near a plane in his life), and by his thirst for whisky and late nights in the back room of the Wheatsheaf.

I was always eager to help on the Commer on Saturdays. Up

at six, I would lay two fires and take tea to my parents in the middle bedroom, where it usually remained undrunk. Then I'd run to the yard where we kept the Commer and the stores. My job was to open up the old stable, and fill and cork two hundred bottles with parazone ready for the coming week.

I'd usually be finishing just as Sid the driver arrived, and we'd load the day's supply of parazone into the Commer on racks behind the passenger seat. Sid would drive us down to the shop. I'd grab some breakfast, and Sid would collect the leather money bag from my mother, who had by this time opened up the shop and taken bacon and eggs to my father upstairs.

We would finish around early evening, and the routine at the end of the day was just as well established. Sid would park on the main road outside the shop, and take the day's money into my parents. My mother and I would count it on the kitchen table, and it was my father's job to go out to the Commer and take a note of the paraffin gauges, and check inside to see what stock had been sold. The routine was changed one Saturday evening, and it was my mother who was killed, not my father as it should have been.

We were back much later than usual. A thick winter's fog was swirling in off the estuary and we had to inch along the lanes. We came in and found my father sitting in front of the wireless. He was filling in the scores on his football coupon, with a half a bottle of whisky on the table beside him. He refused to go out to the van until the results were over. Sid was anxious to get home, and he couldn't take the Commer to the yard until the gauges and stock had been checked. My mother said she would do the checking and that my father would move the van later.

She found a torch, pencil and paper, and went outside. I put the kettle on, went to the bathroom to pee, and chatted to my brother who was splashing about in the bath. I walked through to the front of the house, where I had my bedroom, overlooking the main street. I could only just make out the shape of the Commer, but I could see the fuzzy light from my mother's torch as she checked the gauges. Next thing, the headlights of a car came up behind her. I heard the screech of brakes, like fingers down a blackboard, and then a tremendous bang. The headlights went out, steam came gushing through the fog, and the torch come spinning up towards me.

I ran downstairs. My father was still in the kitchen. I screamed at him and ran out into the fog. I didn't think at all about what I'd find, but wondered what we would do at Christmas.

She was squashed flat against the paraffin tank, her face turned sideways, looking up at the house as if she had tried in that final second to ask for my help. I watched the blood dripping from her mouth, and heard someone retching in the gutter behind me. Neighbours appeared, splashing frantically through the leaking paraffin, and took me away inside.

"Christmas," I said to O'Malley "was a disaster. He took us to a hotel in Cornwall but we ran away with the train tickets and went home. Not bad for two kids in short trousers."

"And fat sausages for ever more?" O'Malley really knew how to put two and two together.

When I arrived home, the house was silent and gloomy. Rachel was in the garden room. I could see she'd been crying. I sat down beside her, and she handed me the *Cambrian News*.

"Page eight," she said, so quietly it was almost a whisper.

At the top of the In Memoriam column was a picture of a black and white collie. The name underneath was Mably, with the words: *Caught in a spinney of murdering herbs.*

"Who could do such a horrible thing?" Rachel asked.

"It's *Milk Wood*, isn't it?"

"Sort of."

"Beynon the butcher?"

"No, Pugh the poisoner."

★　★　★

The day started with slaughter.

I try to let our hens have as much daylight as possible so that they give us lots of eggs in return. I get up about 7-30, and whilst the tea is brewing, I put on my gumboots and walk down to the poultry sheds in my dressing gown and night-shirt. I scoop feed from the bins, and spend a very happy five minutes whilst the ducks, hens and geese scrabble around me fighting for food. And then back for the tea, and upstairs to bed for another hour or so, depending on the weather and the time of year.

I usually let the small birds out first so that they have time for a fair share before their big sisters come running in with their aggressive shrieks and needle-sharp beaks. I opened up the Seebrights, and they came tumbling out of their pop-hole like wild flurries of snow. I unlatched the door to let out the Welsummer bantams but, surprisingly, they didn't emerge. I knelt down and peered into the coop. The five hens lay headless on blood-spattered straw and the young cockerel had wedged himself up near the roof. No fox could have entered the coop so I guessed a stoat had found a small hole in the wire. Not a rat, because rats just chew away at the neck and the eyes, leaving most of the head intact. Stoats and their various relatives, on the other hand, eat the whole head and neck, leaving behind a perfectly formed headless corpse.

No amount of rational argument would persuade us to eat poultry that had been killed by a predator, so I gathered up the hens and put them in a plastic bag, ready for the rubbish collection. I prised the cockerel away from the roof of the coop, and when I put him on the floor I noticed his leg was broken. I would have to kill him.

I went back to the house, poured the tea, and went upstairs where Rachel was already sitting up in bed reading. I told her about the Welsummers and she simply said "Waldo." I said I didn't think so, and explained how the head had been cleanly taken off. No human could do that, I said, but I immediately remembered an incident in a pub in Oxford when I'd seen a student bite off the head of a pigeon as cleanly as any stoat would have done.

Then the phone rang. It was Rosalind Hilton. "I'm coming round to see you," she announced, "it's extremely important."

I was in the shower when she arrived. I heard the bell ring, and then the sound of Rachel and Rosalind talking excitedly together. When I came out, they were in the garden room. Rosalind was sitting on the settee with a bulging plastic bag at her feet, and Rachel was laying out a small breakfast of *pain chocolat*, fruit, and coffee. They were discussing writing and self-discipline, and Rachel was describing the poetry workshop she went to each week.

"Dylan would have found a workshop useful," said Rosalind. "All he had was Vernon." She put down her cup and reached into the plastic bag. She took out a letter and put it on the table.

Rachel recognised the small, cramped handwriting immediately. "It's Dylan," she exclaimed.

"I was lying in bed last night, going through the *Collected Letters*. It made me very angry. It's so unbalanced, just a mere handful of the letters he'd written to women."

"But they were the important women in Dylan's life," I replied, realising too late that that was not the most diplomatic thing to have said. "Caitlin, Edith Sitwell..."

"I've decided to put the matter right," interrupted Rosalind. "This bag holds all of Dylan's letters to me, plus one or two to Waldo. There's also about twenty poems which have never been published, love poems, sent to me, and a few children's stories written for Waldo, though I must say they are a little imperfect and mostly improvised with Waldo on his knee. How you sort them out," she said, looking at Rachel, "is entirely up to you."

"Me?" said Rachel, rather lamely.

"I'd like you to prepare Dylan's letters, and the poems, for publication, as one collection. You're a good poet, you know his work, and I believe you are honest – most Quakers are. And you're Jewish, I like that."

"And your role? asked Rachel.

"You prepare the collection, and we'll work on an introduction together. I can't pay you anything, but you and Waldo can share the royalties."

"And the letters? What's to happen to them?"

"The National Library can have them."

"And time scale?" asked Rachel.

"One that's suitably speedy for an impatient octogenarian who may pop her clogs at any time."

"But why now, after all these years?"

"You're the right person, in the right place, at the right time. Besides..." Rosalind paused and looked across at me "...the conversations with Martin have stirred up too many memories. I need to put a few ghosts firmly in their place."

Rosalind's reply was plausible but I wasn't convinced. I felt that we were being used for some purpose that was being kept from us. Perhaps this was an unworthy thought, but I felt uneasy and certainly not as pleased as Rachel clearly was.

"Here's one I thought you would be particularly interested in," continued Rosalind. "From Dylan's first American trip."

Rachel took the letter, read it with obvious enjoyment, and passed it to me.

> Hotel Earle
> Washington Square
> New York
> 16th May 1950
>
> Oh Rosalind,
>
> I can't begin to tell you how tired I am, & sick like an old dog with mange, sick of this country, sick of trains, sick of planes and Spillanes, sick of poems, sick of not hearing from you, sick in my shoes when I hear my voice in the audit-orium (sic), because my lines are an abacus, and Brinnin counts the money. Did you get the last cheque from Detroit, an awful city where they make motor cars? Did Waldo get the postcard from Seattle? I loved San Francisco! I ran guiltless from the readings to a pub on the water-front called Leprecohens, run by a Jew from Dublin, & read Yeats to fish-oiled sailors who told me stories about Al Catraz. The sea is awash with sardine fleets, and the hills with whizzing cable cars. There is so much to eat, & more to see, in a wonderful clear sunlight, all hills and bridges, slipping down to a bold, blue, coldblew boat-bobbing sea.

I've seen lobsters bigger than cats, & crabs the size of space ships. Cockles are clams & soups are chowders, and women wear pads in their shoulders. I've sucked Baby Ruths and squeezed Tootsie Rolls but I miss Daddie's sexy brown bottles. But the American dream is a nightmare except that the people are not sleeping and will never have the relief of waking up. I have seen men without shoes, beggars without bowls, and Indians with not a bow and arrow between them. It's a moonless, deathfounded night in the back streets, where the eternal poor are spat upon and robbed. Yet I have travelled gloriously: I've met Eisenhower, kissed Ella, played cards with the Duke & heard a scratchy recording of Victoria Spivey, which made my flesh creep and my hair uncurl. I have been to Harlem and back, & wondered why I've never seen Tiger Bay.

Have I mentioned Merle before? Her cousin is a paediatrician, & runs a clinic that could help Waldo. I'm having cocktails with him tomorrow. I will ask Brinnin to put some of my money into an American bank because hospitals here run out of patience if their patients run out of sense. I was stopped in the Bronx last night by a boy no older than Waldo. 'Gimme a dollar,' he said, 'or I scream you to shitsville.' I told him I was an English poet. 'What's so special 'bout poetry,' he rasped, 'just another way of making you poor, right?' I blessed the quality of American education, gave him my autograph and walked on. What a strange word autograph is! The rest of the world is content with a signature.

Merle took me to her Quaker Meeting last Sunday, & I've not been the same since. (Did you know that Caitlin's mother was a lesbian Quaker? Or was she a Quaker lesbian?) We sat down together in a little circle of comfy armchairs, no priests or creed or mumbo-jumbo, & not a cross or crucifix in sight. The silence seemed eternal. Then an old lady started to talk about peace and the coming war. More silence which I drank and drowned in all at once. Then a very intense Negro stood up and spoke for a few minutes about the fate of the Palestinians. As he sat down, he said: 'A mill can't work on the water that has gone'. And that's exactly how I'd been feeling about my writing! How did he know? We all shook hands on the hour, & went off for coffee and gooey cakes in the room next door. They called each other Friend & so they were. If I hadn't had a hangover, I would have been inspired. I was more content than the bottom of a bottle of Buckley's. Do they believe in God? Who knows? Some do, others don't. But they all believe "there's that of God in everyone", even in me! There's hope yet. When I return, I shall have a few more drinks in The Fox and Penn, and ask you how it's possible for a Jew to become a Quaker. Merle did.

I'm bringing a space suit for Waldo, and a hermaphrodite monkey that climbs up a string.

Love, Dylan.

PS. Did Tommy Herbert get the Negro picture magazines?

As I finished reading, Rosalind said: "I'm sure that you'll see this as a labour of love, but you will have to deal with Waldo. He may not approve of the collection, or of you. He's a very private person."

"Have you discussed it with him?"

"No, but I shall inform him this evening." Rosalind stretched out her hand across the coffee table. "Well, Friend, do we have a deal?"

"Let's shake on it," replied Rachel.

I was dispatched to Lampeter to photocopy the papers. It was lunch time when I returned, so we sat outside overlooking the river and ate granary rolls and smoked venison. "I've been thinking about the revelatory power of anomaly," I said between mouthfuls.

"Meaning?"

"Rosalind knew you were a Quaker."

"So?"

"But how did she know? I've never mentioned it."

"Why don't you go and kill that Welsummer. We'll have it for dinner one day."

I did as I was told. The cock was still cowering in the coop. I picked him up and carried him outside so that the other poultry didn't see the dirty deed. I held his body under my right arm, gripped his neck with my left hand and twisted till I heard the snap of his neck. I tied some string around his legs and hung him upside down on a nail, and started plucking. It's easy and therapeutic work when the flesh is warm. When I'd finished, I scooped up the feathers and put them in the rubbish bag with the headless hens. I went inside and laid the bird on the kitchen counter.

I pierced the skin, and cut along the back of the neck, right up to the head. Rachel looked up from Dylan's letters and asked: "Can you do that somewhere else, please?"

"Why did she just suddenly turn up and ask you to work on the papers?"

"I was deeply honoured..."

"But you're a complete stranger. She only met you this morning, but she entrusts her love letters to you." I cut the neckbone with the kitchen secateurs, and pulled off the head and the loose blood vessels, just as the stoat would have done using its teeth. Out came the neckbone. I put my hand inside, loosened the innards and pulled out the gullet.

"She knows my poetry, and she's obviously taken with you..."

"It doesn't make sense." I turned the bird around, cut round the vent, slipped in my hand and pulled gently on the luke-warm intestines until they slithered out across the counter.

"You're too suspicious."

"There's something strange about it." I searched inside for the liver and heart and set them aside for stock. Finally, I pulled out the crop.

"I like her and I trust her."

"I hope you know what you're letting yourself in for." I made a small cut above the feet, snapped the legs down against the edge of the counter, and pulled out the tendons.

"I'll never get another opportunity like this."

"You could get completely caught up in it, spoil your own writing."

"I'll cope."

There was no more to be said. I tied up the legs and wings, and pulled the thread tightly across the parson's nose.

★ ★ ★

I had arranged with Rosalind to have one last interview with her. When I arrived I asked her about Waldo and the letters that she'd given to Rachel. She had told him, and he seemed to have taken the news rather badly. He had tried to persuade her to change her mind. Some of the letters, he had argued, were rightly his, and he did not wish them to be published. It had been left that Rosalind would consider removing these letters but she wanted to discuss the matter with Rachel.

We sat down in front of the fire as usual. "I want to talk about Dylan and his father, because only then will you understand Waldo."

D. J. Thomas, I remembered, was a school teacher for most of his life, contemptuous of his colleagues and pupils and disappointed about not getting a professorship at the university. He had wished to be a poet but in this, too, he was unsuccessful. Dylan bore no physical resemblance whatsoever to DJ, who was taller, and whose features were both more regular and angular.

"History repeats itself, first Dylan and then Waldo."

I didn't understand what she meant, and tried to interrupt but she ploughed on.

"As with the father, so with the son." This was irritating me, but I held my tongue and listened patiently. "When something out-of-the-ordinary happens the first time, we might find it unbelievable. But the second time it happens, it doesn't become more unbelievable at all. On the contrary, we accept it more easily."

"What's this to do with DJ?"

"He wasn't Dylan's father."

"That's ridiculous," I said, and wished immediately I hadn't.

"That's precisely my point. If the same kind of event were to happen a second time, as it did with Waldo, then it becomes more believable."

"Who was Dylan's father, then?" I asked without conviction because I felt no interviewer now, but straight man to Rosalind's funny guy.

"Lord Cut-Glass."

"A Swansea watch-maker?" I asked facetiously.

Rosalind looked at me disapprovingly, as if it were sinful to mock the voices of *Milk Wood*.

"Lord Howard de Walden," she replied.

I was not as really surprised at this as I might have been. After all, there had long been rumours that de Walden was Dylan's real father. He had supported him with money and allowed him to stay at his house in New Quay, and much more besides.

"You see," said Rosalind, interrupting my train of thought, "if you just see him as an aristocrat, then you can't imagine him as Dylan's father. How on earth, you would wonder, did an English aristocrat come to meet Florence Thomas, an unprepossessing Swansea woman married to a school-teacher?"

"That did cross my mind."

"Howard de Walden was a writer, using the family name of Scott-Ellis. It's from him that Dylan inherited his own talent."

And then the penny dropped. Scott-Ellis had been a leading figure in the so-called Celtic revival, just before the First World War, mainly writing operettas. "Did Dylan ever find out about him?"

Rosalind ignored my question but I guessed she would eventually come round to it. "Howard de Walden was a swordsman and hunter, and especially interested in falconry. He liked to invent little tricks for his hawks. His favourite was the German Helmet Call Off. It had started as a prank at a small party he gave towards the end of the war. He invited Dylan to give a reading, and I went with him. No, I left Waldo with my mother.

"To be honest, it was terribly boring. We knew nobody there, which was just as well, I suppose. And Dylan was absolutely furious. The guests behaved rather badly and chatted all the way through his reading.

"When Dylan had finished, one of de Walden's daughters read some Wilfred Owen. She went on a bit too long, and the party were even more restless. De Walden sensed the mood needed changing and announced that he'd fly some peregrines.

There was loud applause. I think people were just bursting with energy after the dreary war years, and poetry wasn't what they wanted. We all went outside except Dylan, who sulked in the Library, drank champagne and ate American chocolate.

"We trooped down to the Hawk House on the lower lawn. De Walden instructed one of the falconers to send the peregrines up. One of the more drunken guests had come out wearing an old German army helmet, the sort with the spike on top. I think it was part of de Walden's military collection in the Great Gallery. De Walden took it from him, and ordered a servant to the kitchen for a cut of sirloin which he then impaled on the spike. He sent the peregrine away, put on the helmet and called the bird back. It came swooping down at tremendous speed. I was absolutely terrified, and some of the women were screaming. I didn't know if de Walden was simply brave or too drunk to notice the danger. Anyway, it turned out fine, and the peregrine took the meat cleanly off the spike.

"Two years later, the autumn of 1946, de Walden was at home. He was expecting friends to call the next morning to buy some young peregrines. There was one that he wasn't sure about, worried it was still a little hood-shy. At the inquest, the butler said that de Walden had decided to go outside and take a last look at the young bird. It was around four in the afternoon and the light was fading. He went out on his own so nobody knows what really happened. Perhaps it was the bad light or an inexperienced bird. Who knows?

"When de Walden hadn't come back to dress for dinner, the butler went out to search for him. He told the inquest that he found de Walden on the ground, and the peregrine beside him, both dead. The coroner deduced he'd been trying the German Helmet Call Off, that the bird had mis-judged it badly and collided with de Walden's head. Its talons had ripped away the side of his face, and the force of the impact had broken his neck. Since then, of course, that particular call off has been banned."

"And Dylan, when did he know about Florence and de Walden?"

"January,1947. He arrived here one day without warning. He was carrying his little doctor's bag, in which he kept the odd clean sock and change of shirt, not much else. When we went upstairs that night, I had to lend him one of my father's old nightshirts – Dylan would never come to bed naked. Anyway, the bag was mostly full of letters. He said he'd been away, had returned to Caitlin at Oxford, there'd been a huge row and he'd walked out, heaping all the letters that had come for him into the bag.

"We went for a long walk along the Aeron, had lunch at the Red Lion in Talsarn and then walked up to the Halt to catch the train home. Sixpence in third class, as I remember. Dylan spent the rest of the afternoon fast asleep upstairs. He came down about five, played with Waldo for a while, fetched a flagon of beer and then emptied his letters on the table. While I cooked dinner, he opened and sorted them into rather untidy piles. I was just about to serve up when I heard a great whoop. I ran into the front room. Dylan was waving a cheque in the air, and shouting 'Bugger me for a saucepan.'

"It was a letter from Howard de Walden's solicitors. Dylan had been named as a beneficiary in de Walden's Will. There was a cheque for £5,000, as well as a sealed envelope which de Walden had instructed his solicitors to send to Dylan along with the legacy. The envelope simply read: 'To Dylan, with affection, Lord Cut-Glass.'

"He opened the envelope tentatively, as if he expected to be taken aback. And he was. The letter was six-pages long, closely typed. He skipped through it and dropped the pages on the table. 'Sweet Lucretia,' he whispered, 'the fowl hears the falcon's bells.'

"We sat in silence whilst he read through the letter again, this time carefully. He poured another beer, picked up the letter, sniffed at it, held it up to the light, rustled it against his good ear and said: 'I'm not a Welsh pervert after all.'

"When I came down from putting Waldo to bed, Dylan handed me the cheque and said 'Buy a farm for him.' And that's what I did, I bought Fern Hill. I think Dylan wanted Waldo to be a real boy, climbing trees, chasing squirrels, that sort of thing.

"Dylan was quiet for most of the evening but more like himself when it was time to go to bed. He clowned around a bit, affecting an even sharper cut-glass accent than he already had: 'Dylan Thomas Esquire, the only son and heir of Lord Howard de Walden,' he said, lifting up his night-shirt, 'at your service ma'am.'

"I'd say he was bewildered more than shocked but it didn't last. That's the thing about Dylan, the outer world didn't touch him for long and he was soon his old self. In fact, I saw him scribbling some verses, the first for more than two years. 'Some lines for my new pater, and his birds', he said. That was the start of 'Over Sir John's hill' but he soon lost interest. The next year he wrote 'Me and My Bike'."

"Meaning?"

Rosalind gave me a withering look. "It's an operetta," she said, and I felt the cold wind of exasperation on my face. "Don't you see?"

I nodded.

"Like father, like sunbeam. The fuse was blue not green, and Dylan flowered thereafter."

"Did he tell Caitlin?"

"Yes, but she didn't believe him. She thought it was one of his stories again, and he couldn't show her the letter without explaining where the money had gone. Anyway, she loathed de Walden, something one of his ancestors had done in Ireland."

"Did he say anything to DJ and his mam?"

"Of course not. What was the point?"

"Did it change his relationship with DJ?"

"They became much closer. Not so much father and son but good friends. They did more together, doing the crossword... the attachment grew but I had the feeling that Dylan felt freer, not of DJ and the family, but free of his Welsh baggage, if you like."

"But he settled in Laugharne."

"That was part of it. Once he felt free of being Welsh, he felt comfortable about settling in Wales, and not being brought down by the bits he despised. The letter helped him understand why he felt such an outsider in Wales, he stopped feeling guilty about it. It also made him more detached, turned him into an observer, and that really helped *Under Milk Wood* to develop, and the later poetry, too."

I wanted to move on. "Can we talk about Dylan's mother?"

"He spoke little about Florence." Rosalind paused as though she were making a judgement about the wisdom of what she was about to say. "Children usually have a very narrow view of their parents, so when a surprise comes along it affects the way they see the world generally, not just the parent. And I think that's what happened to Dylan. The Cut-Glass letter put Florence in a whole new light, and that made Dylan see his Welsh world differently. The Welsh weren't perverts anymore but eccentrics, full of colour and light, a rich people behind the grey conformities, individualists and nonconformists in the real sense. That's why there are so many wonderful characters in *Milk Wood*. I don't think Dylan would have divined them without the impact of de Walden's revelations about Florence. And Caitlin's abortion, of course."

Rosalind had a knack off going off on a tangent to her main story, and I felt she enjoyed being tantalising. I decided to stay focused and come back to Caitlin's abortion later.

"Did de Walden say how the affair began?"

"I think 'affair' is wrong, it was more a brief fling."

"How did they meet?"

"In Swansea, in 1912."

"But how?"

"You see, you're thinking de Walden again. Don't think horse-breeding, falcon-flying aristocrat. Think Scott-Ellis, think Welsh-speaking song writer and minor poet. Think Scott-Ellis and you think of someone who loved Welsh culture and the language as much as Florence's cantankerous DJ despised them."

"Think Florence...."

"And you think of someone who was warm and generous, who loved talking and company, unlike DJ who never invited anyone into the house in all the time they were there. They lived separate lives. He had his books and a pint or two every night.

She had the kitchen, her friends from chapel and the nights at the Grand, where her gaiety was given full rein. He was bookish and intellectual, but Florence was shrewd and intelligent, and people often made the mistake of under-estimating her, sometimes to their cost.

"Florence was born and brought up in Swansea, she was an urban child, and far more cosmopolitan than DJ. She knew more about the real world. He knew nothing much of modern times save what he learnt from Lawrence and Hemingway. She was inquisitive and searching, and knew about the great capital cities. She'd never visited them, of course, but her father was a railwayman who had worked his way up to Inspector. He'd been all over, including the Orient Express, and his stories filled her mind with the excitement of travel and the wonder of life outside Wales."

"So tell me how they met."

"Howard de Walden – Scott-Ellis – went to Swansea in 1912 to collaborate with Dr Vaughan Thomas, setting traditional Welsh poems to music. Vaughan Thomas and DJ were good friends, as were their sons later, and that was how Florence met de Walden. There were tea parties at the Vaughan Thomases, and outings to the beach when the weather permitted. All this is in the Cut-Glass letter, by the way. In 1914, just after Christmas, de Walden came back to Swansea to stage a minor opera at the Grand, and there met Florence again. The Grand was her abiding passion, much looked down upon by DJ who could never understand why a theatre was necessary when you could read Shakespeare from a book and recite it aloud, if needs be.

"Florence was one of the volunteers who helped out back stage. She'd been a seamstress before she met DJ, so she helped in making up the costumes."

"Did she act?"

"I think she'd have liked to but that would have brought a sharp word from the deacons."

"Dylan was a great play-actor..."

"He had a wonderful sense of theatre, and it was from Florence that it came. His acting ability came from her, too, and most of his voice power. Even in old age, she had a rich, wonderful voice."

"So the Grand was the opportunity, and perhaps the place," I said, "but what was the motive?"

"By which you mean?"

"Why did they fall for each other?"

"We can only guess, the Cut-Glass letter tells us nothing on that score. De Walden and Florence were much younger than DJ, of course, who was entering middle-age. In fact, he'd been middle-aged most of his life, bald at twenty-six, sitting down to meals in his hat, and even going to bed in it. De Walden, on the other hand, was not only young but well-travelled. He'd been on a late-Victorian version of the Grand Tour and could regale Florence about Florence, and all the other cities that she had heard about from her father. And they could do all this in Welsh, which DJ had become more and more reluctant to use.

"Then there's the question of sex. Both DJ and Florence had enlightened views on that. When they married, she was already pregnant, but the baby was lost soon after. Then Nancy was born but it was another eight years before Dylan came along. Was there something amiss in the marriage bed? Was Florence desperate for another baby? Who can tell?

"It was often said that DJ had married below himself, and I'm sure Florence thought so at times. Catching de Walden must have been a great confidence-booster. It was also a way of thumbing her nose at DJ for his insufferable superiority. He may have thought she was only good for warming his slippers, but she now knew she could get on with the toffs, and even fall into bed with one.

"I suspect she found a kindred soul in de Walden who didn't despise her gaiety and simple love of life in the way that DJ did. I think she wanted affection, she wanted respect and, of course, a more sociable life than DJ could offer. She only really came into her own after DJ and Dylan had both died. She blossomed, showing the tourists around Laugharne, being Dylan's Mam. She loved meeting people, telling the stories about Dylan, making fun of the Americans, showing where the grave was, because that was all the Japanese wanted to see...poor Flo, she lost her husband, son and daughter all within the space of eleven months."

"But she was chapel. Would she really have allowed herself to fall for de Walden?"

"The Welsh weren't so prim and proper, you know. That's what made Carodoc Evans so angry, the hypocrisy, the chapel elders, Bible in one hand, the key to Rosie Probert's bedroom in the other, and heading for the backroom of the pub on Sunday nights."

"But a Lord and a schoolmaster's wife? Chirk Castle and number 5, Cwmdonkin Drive?"

"Since when has a contumescent man enquired which school one has been to? Did Eliot worry about screwing a Jew? Did he make his excuses and leave?"

"But..." I stumbled, shaken by the power and frankness of this old woman's language.

"No buts. You know all this. Weren't you the one who wrote a thesis on the sexual behaviour of the British aristocracy? And what did you find?"

She was right, but I was rigid with shock. How did she know? I'd written that thesis in 1968, in between times, whilst I helped organise the Vietnam war demonstrations at the London School of Economics. How could she possibly have found out? And why had she bothered? Waldo's puppy tails were nothing to this.

"Anyway, she let de Walden know that she was pregnant but that she wanted to hear nothing more from him whatsoever, and certainly never to see him again. DJ apparently assumed the baby was his, and perhaps it was. Who knows? But de Walden did write once, just to say that he had written an opera, that it was called *Dylan, Son of the Wave*, and might the opera be dedicated to the child, if it were a boy, as a token of de Walden' appreciation of the friendship and hospitality he had received in Swansea? The letter was addressed to both DJ and Florence, and written, I imagine, in the most circumspect terms. Florence wrote back on behalf of DJ and herself. Her husband, she said, had no views on the matter of a name, but she herself would be delighted, if it were a boy, to call him Dylan."

Rosalind stopped, and went to the kitchen to make some tea. I sat in a rather sombre mood by the fire, still puzzled by her reference to my thesis. She was quite right, of course. There had been a considerable weakening in the economic position of the aristocracy in Victorian times. They had compensated by marrying their children into the new wealth of industry and finance. Partly as a result, social conventions became much less exacting. Peers and their sons were permanent fixtures at theatre doors, and they were marrying singers and actresses by the score. What happened between de Walden and Florence at the Grand Theatre, I mused, was not an extraordinary event, but an insignificant moment in a process of wider social change.

I heard the sound of someone sobbing in one of the bedrooms upstairs. It sounded like the crying of a young child in a hospital ward late at night. Not the tears of pain or neglect, but loneliness.

Rosalind came back into the room carrying a tray with tea and some food. "Imitation sausage rolls," she said, putting the tray on the table between us. "Dylan came unexpectedly one day, and I had nothing to give him. So I invented these. Not real sausage because you couldn't get that in the war. Just cold haricot beans, put through the mincer with a bit of cold meat, a rasher of bacon, lots of pepper and sage, some herbs, and then well pounded."

I thought of Mr Beynon and Mr Pugh.

Rosalind passed the plate across. "I hope you like them, Martin."

I looked at the plate. There were two rows of thin sausages, not sausage rolls at all, because they had no pastry. "You made them the right size for me."

"Go ahead, you must be hungry."

"No, please, after you. I'll have some tea first."

She took a sausage from the row nearest to her, and put the

plate back on the table so that the full row was closest to me. "Now, where were we?"

"How did you find out about my thesis?" I had meant to ask why had she gone to so much trouble but she understood what I was really after.

"You think I'd have these talks with you without first doing my homework?"

"But it's from such a long time ago."

"It's all on the Net." She let the pause tease me. "Don't look so surprised. This old lady knows how to surf."

I heard the creak of a bed. I wondered if it would be polite to ask who was upstairs.

"You still haven't had a sausage."

"In a minute."

"There's some sorrel in them and one or two things from Fern Hill." She took another sausage from her side of the plate. She fixed her gaze on me, willing me, or so I felt, to take one. "All that trouble I took to make them."

I could hear crying again from upstairs. Either Rosalind heard nothing or she was determined to ignore it and pretend everything was normal. She stood up, and went to the kitchen to re-fill the tea-pot. I snatched up a sausage from my side of the plate, and put it in my jacket pocket. She came back into the room with the fresh tea. "That was lovely," I said, smacking my lips, "best sausage I've had since O'Malley's."

"Let's get back to *Under Milk Wood*."

This is *Milk Wood*, I thought.

"You see, it hasn't got much of a plot, it depends totally on character revelation, and Dylan didn't see the characters until he'd seen the identical ambiguities of his own and Waldo's conception. And that's precisely where the play comes unstuck. It's hopelessly unbalanced..."

"Too much sex..."

"No, that's what they all get wrong. Dylan was obsessed with *paternity*."

I heard the bed creak again, followed by the sound of

someone shuffling across the floor.

"You may not have realised..." pausing as if telling me to brace myself for some startling information, "...but *Milk Wood* contains six menage à trois, numerous fatherless babies, three loose women and even more looser men, all neatly tied symbolically together in Mr Waldo's many paternity summonses."

"And Dylan saw himself as both Mr Waldo senior and little Waldo his son?"

"Yes, the bastard who begot another."

"And Lord Cut-Glass, whose letter made the genius flower?"

"The time lord, tending his sixty-six clocks, one for each year of de Walden's life. The clues are there if you want to find them."

I heard someone upstairs quietly clearing their throat.

"And DJ's in there too, the tidy, anal, bullying personality, the obsession with cleanliness, the refusal to allow visitors into the house..."

"Mrs Ogmore-Pritchard." I said confidently. I decided it was time to explore another path: "You mentioned Caitlin's abortion earlier."

"Dylan had great trouble with *Under Milk Wood*. The news about Florence and de Walden started the ideas flowing, but it only really fell into place after Caitlin's abortion in 1951. Beynon the butcher was really Beynon the abortionist, that was the name of the doctor who did it. And that's how Caitlin described it, like being in a butcher's shop. The foetus was six-months, a perfectly formed baby. The doctor had to cut it up to get it out, pulling the baby out in chunks, Mr Beynon's chops, bits of leg and arm everywhere. The awful thing was Caitlin only had it done so that she could go with Dylan to America."

"It's a bit shocking, killing a six-month foetus like that."

"At least *Milk Wood* was born of it even if the baby wasn't."

There were footsteps on the stairs. This time, Rosalind heard them. "Don't worry, it's only Waldo. He's been rather poorly, since I told him about Rachel doing Dylan's letters."

I imagined him quiet on the stairs, crouching low to catch the conversation, like a small child listening to the grown-ups talking late at night. The latch of the stairwell door clicked open. Rosalind looked across and said: "Come in Waldo, it's only Mr Pritchard."

I looked apprehensively across the room. Waldo was standing at the foot of the stairs, hunched up inside a voluminous dark blue night-shirt. He seemed to have shrivelled, and shrunk so small that he wasn't the man I had seen at Fern Hill. I remembered his dark, wavy hair that night when I had watched him at his desk, but now it was greasy and matted, and stuck out like spikes from his head. His white face was puffed up in blotches, and his nose was covered in spots of blood as if he'd been scratching it in his sleep. His left eye was bloodshot and the skin below badly bruised. He looked distraught, and stared helplessly at his elderly mother who at that moment seemed twenty years younger than him. She radiated energy whilst he looked empty and pathetic.

Rosalind beckoned him to cross the room. "Come and meet Mr Pritchard, Waldo."

I forced a smile that said hello. Waldo stared at me, his bloodshot eye watering down his cheek.

I got up from my chair and took a few steps towards him, stretching out my hand. "I'm pleased to...."

"Must the hawk in the egg kill the wren?" he asked.

"Sorry?"

"Will the fox in the womb kill more chickens?"

There seemed no point in staying. I drove home and parked the car outside the house. I felt in my jacket pocket for the key to the front door, but my fingers found only Rosalind's sticky sausage. I withdrew it carefully from my pocket and threw it on the ground, and next door's cat came rushing through the hedge and carried it away.

Fast Forward 2

Rebel against the flesh and bone,
The word of the blood, the wily skin,
And the maggot no man can slay.

"This ear that you're worried about," said the Inspector, pushing the last corner of an egg sandwich into his mouth.

"It's gone to forensic, sir."

"Who actually found it?"

"Mrs Watkins Kingdom Hall," replied the Sergeant, politely turning away as the Inspector scraped bits of bread from between his teeth with the sharp end of a paper clip.

"And where exactly did she come across it?"

"In the pull-in by the Scadan Coch."

"And whose ear is it?"

"A man's ear, sir. Right side."

"Any distinguishing features?"

"Someone's taken a large bite out of it."

"And how was it detached from its owner?"

"Sharp blade, sir, like a razor."

"Anything else?"

"This was pinned to it," replied the Sergeant, passing across a stained post-it note wrapped in a polythene bag.

*"*Before death takes you, O take back this,*" read the Inspector. "Mean anything to you?"*

"Afraid not, sir."

"Perhaps we should call in the Poet Laureate, then. To get the case going, to set things in motion," suggested the Inspector, knowing it was wasted. *"Doesn't your auntie have any views on the matter?"* he asked, trying to soften the bite in his voice.

"She always said that God has the hymns, and the Devil has the poetry."

"From the maniac's tongue pours deathfilled singing."

"You've lost me there, sir."

"Browning, the wife," responded the Inspector, sighing loudly. "We have a murderer who knows his poems."

"And is a bit of a butcher."

"To whom does the ear in question belong?"

"Can't say, sir. We've checked the hospitals and doctors. Nothing missing from the mortuary, either."

"No pub brawls or dirty work in the scrum?"

"Not that we've been able to ascertain."

"And no-one's come in and reported their ear's gone missing?"

"No, sir."

"Or that of a close relative?"

"No, sir."

"Well, Sergeant, you'd better start looking for a body, then."

"Murder, sir?"

"Foul play of some kind."

That of Satan

Rachel woke up late and grumpy. I made some tea, let out the poultry and got back into bed. When I started talking about Waldo, yet again, she sharply reminded me I had a fledgling business to attend to. I left her reading *Lives of Great Quakers* and headed into Lampeter. The office was much as I'd left it, though the cleaner had piled the junk mail onto my chair, and pinned the Diana Dors photograph above the desk. There were three messages on the answer machine. The moral philosophy tutor wanted to know what progress I'd made in finding Dylan's shed. A young woman from Cardiff asked me to search for her husband whom she'd lost on the coastal footpath several years ago. An Action Group in a nearby village wondered if I would discreetly investigate a local farmer. I rang the secretary. She told me they were worried that he was running trials on genetically modified rape. They wanted to know who his financial backers were. They couldn't pay me but promised a turkey for Christmas.

As I put the phone down, Waldo walked through the door. He looked much better, but I could see he was angry. I offered him a seat. He pushed it away, and leaned across my desk. "What the hell you up to?"

I moved my chair back to escape the foul smell on his breath. "I'm trying to find Dylan's shed," I replied, wondering what he'd been eating.

"Bugger the shed."

"It belongs to you."

"So do his letters."

"Your mother wants them published."

"I can do that myself."

"The decision's been made."

"Over my dead body."

"You don't understand..."

"But I do. Your wife wants a bit of fame at my expense."

"It's a labour of love. She's not being paid."

Waldo looked at me intently. He reached in his coat pocket, took out a little pearl-handled knife and started digging the dirt from behind his nails. "Love's labours are sometimes better lost," he eventually said. "Too many tears, too much bloo..."

"It's too late," I interrupted. "They're in the National Library. Rachel's working from copies."

"You had no right."

"They belong to the nation now."

"You've robbed me of my past."

"It could give you a future."

"It's not what I want at my age," he shouted angrily, banging his fist on the desk.

"I think it's time you went."

"I think," he replied, as he moved towards the door, "it's time you started taking me seriously."

He left, slamming the door hard behind him. I sharpened a few pencils and called my brother at New Scotland Yard, and asked him if there was anything on the files for Rosalind and Waldo. He coughed and spluttered, and muttered about losing his job but eventually promised to do what he could. In fact, he rang me back almost immediately. A good deal on Waldo, he said, from an early age: truancy, stealing, fighting, driving and taking away, grievous bodily harm, and damaging property in the National Library of Wales. Rosalind's 'form' was altogether more interesting. She'd been arrested with Ian Fleming in a high security zone outside a sensitive military establishment. They'd been enjoying themselves on the back seat of Fleming's Lanchester. Fleming had punched the security guards but strings were pulled and no charges were brought, though both were closely questioned by Military Intelligence.

"When did this happen?" I asked.

"Summer, 1950."

"Anything else?"

"There are a couple of Special Branch cross-refs. Visits abroad, I think, but I daren't check."

"Any advice?"

"Stay well clear."

I rang the National Library. Oh, yes, they certainly remembered Waldo Hilton.

"A voracious reader?" I asked.

"Not quite. He came in about two years ago, asked for a day ticket, and ordered all of T.S.Eliot's books. The Reading Room was almost empty, it was August, and the staff weren't watching the security monitors. It was our fault, really. Anyway, he took out this package, put it on the table and started slicing it up with a scalpel. To be fair, someone on the desk did eventually see it and she was just about to go and tell him that food wasn't allowed in the Reading Room, when the phone rang and she forgot all about it. Except it wasn't food. It was a giant turd, which he was slicing up and putting between the pages of Eliot's books. It's all on the video tape, if you want to see it. We use it for induction training all the time."

I decided it was time for a drink and drove back to the Scadan Coch. The pub was quiet, unusually for the time of year. Billy Logs was sitting on the bench next to the bar, cleaning his chainsaw whilst he waited for his food. Miss Price Rose Cottage was sitting opposite, feeding peanuts to her dog and occasionally throwing some across to Llewela, though I doubted that this was a proper snack for a miniature llama. Next to Miss Price sat Dai Dark Horse, who ran the fishing and barber shop in the village. This had always struck me as a curious combination and it wasn't always clear what customers were waiting for. Someone asking for a Number Two could just as well be referring to a type of hook as to a cropped haircut. When Dai asks "Anything for the weekend?" the answer is as likely to be a can of worms as a pack of condoms. It's certainly disconcerting to be sitting in the barber's chair when a customer asks for maggots. Dai puts down the scissors and goes into the back room where the tubs of maggots are stored. I know he wears rubber gloves and washes his hands but it's still a very uncomfortable feeling when he comes back to work on your hair.

O'Malley was sitting on a high stool behind the bar, embroidering a sampler depicting the celebration in the pub on the night we voted for a Welsh Assembly. O'Malley's embroidery brought as many customers to the pub as his food, and most came just to marvel that a man with only two fingers on his left hand could embroider so beautifully. The pub walls were decorated with his samplers, as were the covers for the tables, each of which contained verses from his favourite poets. They were covered with heavy plate glass, and they gave the pub something of the atmosphere of a Dutch café.

O'Malley was too engrossed in his needlework to care much about his customers, so I went behind the bar, took a bottle of Brains and helped myself to some toad-in-the-hole made with sliced pigeon breasts. O'Malley grunted and pointed with his chin towards the end of the counter, indicating that the toad would not be complete without some beetroot jelly and a spoonful of pickled nasturtium seeds. He was right.

The discussion in the bar was animated. One of the area's striking characteristics is the large number of holly trees in the woods. The principal reason for this is that Billy Logs, like his father before him, refuses to cut down holly trees because to do so would bring a lifetime of bad luck and pestilential curses. Dai was teasing him about this but was making a serious point about the unbalanced nature of the local woodland. I tucked into my toad and listened to the talk, which is perhaps why I was the first person to hear the car.

Then O'Malley looked up, clearly not pleased with the prospect of further customers at this moment. We heard four doors slamming in quick succession, and the ostentatious click of central locking, followed by the beep of the alarm being activated. Just as the door opened we heard a small child say: "But *why* can't we go to Macdonalds?" Llewela instantly stood to attention. We waited nervously, because the level of English decibel at which she was likely to spit was never predictable.

70

The family that came into the bar were largely what I had expected. Mr and Mrs Volvo and their two children stood for a moment on the threshold. We stopped talking immediately because that is the respectful custom, is it not, when strangers enter a pub deep in the Welsh countryside. It's the polite thing to do, but people often misunderstand. Miss Price smiled, and the conversation started again.

Mr Volvo led the family to the bar. "I gather you serve food here?"

We waited to see how O'Malley would react. His prejudices were finely honed so he had no one particular way of dealing with English-speaking customers. He picked a response according to the occasion, the customer, how he was generally feeling about the world and whether or not his love life with Ringle, the coxswain from New Quay, was still intact. He put his needlework on the bar, glanced up but said nothing. Mr Volvo looked puzzled but it could have been irritation because the two children were tugging impatiently at his green and baggy corduroy trousers.

"Do you have a menu?" asked Mrs Volvo, raising her voice as if she were on the Continent. Llewela cocked her ear but stayed quiet.

O'Malley reached across with two menus. "*Croeso*," he said.

The family retreated to the Philip Larkin table near the window. They read the menu, then read it again, and finally turned it over, looking for an English translation. "I suppose its lasagne and chips again, it's what they usually have down here."

The conversation dropped a little and I saw O'Malley prise himself off the high stool. I knew he didn't care about the lasagne and chips, but he'd be furious about "it's what they have down here." It makes you wonder why people come to Wales on holiday. Last month, a group of English tourists signed up for an evening of traditional Welsh song and entertainment at the summer *eisteddfod*. They walked out during the interval, complaining that it was all in Welsh, and demanding their money back. The organisers gave it to them. Some thought this was wimpish and said the tourists should have been ejected. But one of the marvellous things about the Welsh is their politeness even in the face of extreme provocation.

Mr Volvo got up and walked to the bar. "So sorry, but do you have an English menu?"

"This is a Welsh speaking establishment."

Mr Volvo looked momentarily taken aback, but responded very heartily: "Don't speak it, old boy."

Llewela twitched and O'Malley leaned across the bar. "What would you do in France?"

"My wife speaks perfect French."

"In Italy, then, or Spain or Germany..."

Mr Volvo hesitated and his wife called across: "We'd have a phrase book, wouldn't we?"

"And where's your Welsh phrase book, then?"

"But you all speak English, for goodness sake."

"So they do in Holland but you'd still take your phrase book with you."

"Mummy went to Dutch classes last year," chipped in the oldest child.

"Our anniversary, you know, had a wonderful fortnight in Amsterdam," squirming all the way down from the neck of his Arran sweater to the soles of his Timberland boots.

"I wonder if you'd be kind enough to translate," asked Mrs Volvo, leaving the table and joining her husband at the bar.

"That's another thing," said O'Malley. "Abroad, you'd ask the waiter to translate, wouldn't you. But why not here?"

"English is the language of commerce, old chap."

"Darling, let me deal with this..."

Fellow!

O'Malley heard the missing word as surely as the rest of us. Llewela stood up.

"Now look here, we've been hours on the M4, the children are starving..."

"Lobscouse," said O'Malley.

"I beg your pardon."

"A Danish stew. Beef, potato and bayleaf."

"I'm a veggie, actually."

"Then there's potato dumplings and beetroot in sour sauce."

"And for the children?"

O'Malley turned, and looked across to the table where the children were sitting: "What d'you fancy?"

What a saint O'Malley could be!

"Chips," said the younger child, smiling defiantly at her mother.

"With?" asked O'Malley.

"Lasagne," replied her brother.

"You got it," said O'Malley, disappearing into the kitchen, beaming with delight.

The Volvos sat back around the table. We carried on talking about holly, they began discussing the merits of various schools in Islington. The children fidgeted, bored and hungry but gave O'Malley, whom we'd never seen so tolerant of English in the bar, a big smile when he brought the knives and forks to the table. I took my cue from O'Malley, and smiled at Mrs Volvo. "My brother's son," I said, "did very well at Acland Burghley Comprehensive."

She looked at me in astonishment. "Isn't it rather cosmopolitan?" she asked.

"Look, mummy, there's a camel in the corner," said the boy.

"Ssh, James, I'm talking to the nice gentleman..."

"So you're from London?" said Mr Volvo, brightening up. "On holiday?"

"But mummy, there's a camel..."

"No, I live in the village."

"Not a camel, darling, a baby llama."

"We hope to buy a cottage down this way."

"It's so important to take the children out of London now and again, don't you think?"

"What's this say, mummy?" asked the girl, pointing at the Larkin poem on the embroidered cloth that covered their table.

"Why Wales?" I asked.

"I'm sorry?"

"Why choose Wales for your cottage?"

"Perhaps you've relations here," suggested Billy Logs, walking towards the door, with the chainsaw dangling from his immense fist.

"What does it say, mummy?" asked the young child in frustration.

"We did try Herefordshire," said Mr Volvo.

"But the prices were simply outrageous," added his wife.

"I'll read it for you," offered her elder brother helpfully.

"Bet you can't."

"So it's just the prices then?"

"Sorry?"

"Choosing Wales."

"And the motorway to Carmarthen, it only takes four hours..."

"Go on then, read it, if you're so clever."

"But not the people," I asked, "not the history, the scenery...?"

"Oh, of course, that too..."

"We rather like Dylan Thomas," added Mr Volvo smugly.

"It rhymes with 'duck'," I said, "not with 'dill'."

"Duck in a dill and caper sauce. There's an idea for you," said O'Malley, appearing with the condiments.

"I'll read it backwards for you."

"Show off."

"*And add some extra, just for you.*"

"Mummy, when's the chips coming?"

"*They fill you with the faults they had.*"

"Your nephew liked Acland Burghley?"

"*They may not mean to, but they do.*"

"So it's the prices then..."

"But certainly not the Prices," interjected Miss Price, nimbly.

"Sorry?"

"*They fuck you up, your Mum and Dad.*"

"James!" shrieked Mrs Volvo.

Llewela came rushing across from the bar. She stopped next to the Volvo's table. Her ears were twitching, and her mouth was stretched in a grimace of effortless superiority that only llamas and chemists know how to make.

"I'd stay quiet, if I were you," I advised, "otherwise she's likely to spit at you."

O'Malley emerged from the kitchen with a tray laden with food. He sent Llewela back to her basket, unloaded the plates and asked the Volvos what they'd like to drink.

"And have you found anywhere to buy?" asked Dai Dark Horse.

"We've only just started looking," replied Mrs Volvo, still watching Llewela nervously, and even more apprehensively at her son.

"There's a place we're going to see later," said Mr Volvo.

"Fern Hill," added his wife.

Now it was my turn to be shocked. It was less than two weeks since I had last seen Waldo and Rosalind but I'd heard nothing about the farm being up for sale. "It's just down the road," I said. "Needs a bit of work, lots of character, though."

"Did you know that Dylan Thomas was Bob Dylan's real father?" asked Mrs Volvo.

"I'm sure you're right," I replied, nodding my head sagely to humour her. It was the stalest of old chestnuts. Such stories were forever blowing in the wind down here.

Mr Volvo stood up and held out his arm. "Stillness," he said, taking my hand and shaking it vigorously. "Ogmore Stillness. Perhaps we'll be neighbours soon."

The next time I saw Ogmore Stillness, he was lying face down in the Aeron, the sleeve of his Arran sweater snagged on a branch of blackthorn brought low in the river by the sloe-backed weight of its own fruitfulness.

I walked home, and found Rachel at the kitchen table becalmed on a sea of photocopied letters. She had finished the main sorting of the material that Rosalind had left. There were twelve poems by Dylan, mostly undated; over a hundred letters from May 1949 to October 1953; a handful of postcards from Prague and Sussex; and six short stories written for, or about, Waldo, which Rachel felt should be published separately. Of all the things on the table, my favourites were the flotsam and jetsam from the Scadan Coch, upon which Dylan had scribbled fragments of poems, including an early draft of 'Poem on His Birthday', written on the inside of a packet of Sweet Afton.

"Here's Dylan's first letter to Rosalind from America," said Rachel.

I took the letter and stared in some wonderment at the crumpled handwriting:

Midston House
22 East 38th Street
New York 16
Saturday, 25th February 1950

My dear Rosalind,

A long and ghastly plane trip, & then heaved Brinnin-ho into an audience of 800 people, and afterwards a grasping, clasping, fawning reception in an apartment (flat) large enough to hold the parish of Ciliau & all its cows, whose intelligence I sorely miss. Brinnin is the archetypal Thief, whip-cracking my time and sanity through a collideascope of dotty bow-ties and snakeskin handbags. Eminent professors push knock-eyed wives at me, doctoral students hang on every gallowed word (oh, that they would till their lips were blue) and dull and desperate dentists ask me gum-numbing questions about our new national health service. They quiz me about Aneurin Bevin and Ernie Bevan, & are they brothers, they ask. I promise them that Mr Attlee will bring clement weather, & that Beveridge is not a bedtime drink. I now at last understand politics: the Germans are cuckoos, the Italians are song thrushes, the English are wrens and the Americans pigeons. I miss you so, and wish you and Waldo were here so that we could hold each other in silence and let this country's banshee noise wash through my head till only the splash of your feet kicking through the Aeron remains.

Tell that Dylan-loined lion of ours that I have drunk

milkshakes in cafés called drugstores, eaten hamburgers
made from beef, sucked chips as thin and tasteless as
wooden swans, & been sick into the hat of a very small lady
who stood in front of me at the top of the Empire State
Building (what Empire?) as it, or I, swayed in the wind. I
shall eat beans with deans, scones with dons and swill
Californian wine fermented from chinese dragon tongues.

They want a poet here but I cannot, for the life or
death of me, give them one. The muse has donkeyed into
the desert. My peregrine genes are exploding like over-ripe
zucchini (marrows?). Hello Scott-Ellis, come and get me
Harry Parr Davies. Shout theatre, scream movies (cinema),
trumpet television (is there one in Ciliau yet – you must go
and see it. I'm sure Tyglyn will have one) – these are to be
the bottle-bright milkmen of my waterfalling words. Soon I
shall be a great writer of opera, too. Walton is keen to work
with me, Auden's hinted at Stravinsky. They murmur here
about war in Korea, but I shall have my career from it.
From liberation to libretti. Milk Wood is festering nicely,
too, and Gossamer Beynon sends her regards. I must now
get ready for another reading. I have to change my pants
(trousers), take the elevator (lift) and telephone for a cab
(taxi), though it would be quicker to walk (eccentric).
The city is choked with automobiles (cars) and my chest is
daily tightening in the smog. I must do something about it,
but I loathe quacks, and where would the time come from?
On my redgravestone, please put: "He died because he was
never long enough in one place to have it seen to" (joke). I
rest tomorrow, and then readings at Yale and Harvard, & a
reading a day thereafter until May 18th. I shall see all
America fast asleep.

Love,

Dylan.

PS I'm sending Waldo some American comics. And lots of
chocolates & candy (sweets) for his birthday. I'm a fat,
sweating, aching beetroot. Oh, Rosalind, what am I doing
here? I want to lie quietly with you in love & peace. Rustle
your petticoats on the banks of the Aeron & send me the
sound in a vase (vase).

I hovered a while over the letters until I was clucked at to go away. "There was a man called Stillness in the pub," I said, putting the kettle on, "with his barboured family. He's thinking of buying Waldo's place."

"It's up for sale?"

"Apparently."

"Why?"

"That's what I asked O'Malley."

"And his two-fingered opinion?"

"That Waldo's not been the same since the shed was stolen."

"Or since you started interviewing his mother."

"With your encouragement, I remember."

"We've an agreed joint project here, Martin. You interview Rosalind and find Dylan's shed, I edit the papers. It's a very important piece of work for me."

"Have you wondered," I asked, "why there aren't any letters before May 1949? That was when Dylan and Caitlin moved to Laugharne."

★ ★ ★

Appropriately enough, we met by chance in Conti's café in Lampeter. I'm an ice cream addict and Leno Conti makes one of the best in the world.

Rosalind was sitting at one of the tables near the door, eating a boiled egg with precision-cut soldiers soaked in garlic butter. I slid across the plastic bench already incised by two generations of teenage denim studs. Leno came across with a *caffè macchiato* and a bowl of ice cream covered in blueberries.

"Boiled egg, the Italian way?" I asked, as Rosalind crunched into the last of her pieces of bread.

"I've always liked the Italians."

"Italians are Jewish," I said, remembering an old Lenny Bruce routine.

"Only northern Italians."

"There was never ice cream as good as this in Italy."

"Dylan liked his covered in Sambuca."

"I didn't think you could get either during the war."

"Not here you couldn't. But this was afterwards."

"The Tuscany trip?"

"He hated every minute. Much too hot for a fat man. And the beer was too cold."

"When was this?"

"1947. He took the whole family, and Caitlin's sister Brigit. He hated Florence, too many thin-lipped intellectuals, he said."

"So why did he go?"

"MI6 sent him. They were worried about the communists on Elba. Did you know," Rosalind said, cracking the empty eggshell between her fingers, "that even the policemen wore badges of Lenin on their uniforms?"

"To spy on the politicians? Is that why Dylan went?"

"No, much more serious than that. Elba had huge deposits of iron ore. It used to go to the works at Portoferraio for processing but after the war Italsider, the owners, closed it down. So all the ore had to be shipped to the mainland. We had intelligence reports that large quantities of it were being siphoned off by the Elba workers to the Soviet Union. Something to do with extracting uranium for the hydrogen bomb."

"Why Dylan?"

"Elba was a closed community, especially Rio Marina, where the ore was being shipped from. We needed someone to pave the way. Dylan was perfect for the job. He could get on with virtually everybody, and he knew something about mining. Not a lot, but enough. One of his best friends at New Quay, Evan Joshua, had managed the quarry there. And Killick, of course, had worked in the mines in Africa. It was enough for us to build on. And his obsession with Auden, of course."

"Sorry?"

"All that stuff in *The Prophets* about lead mining."

"But Dylan didn't speak Italian."

"Caitlin spoke some, and Brigit was fluent. And remember, Dylan didn't need words to communicate."

Rosalind paused whilst Leno Conti put a plate of almond biscuits on the table. "The plan was for Dylan to make sufficient contacts in Florence to get an introduction to Elba. We knew that going in cold wouldn't work. Once he was on the island, Ian Fleming and I – and Waldo of course – would join him. Fleming was still working for MI6, though he was on the staff of the *Sunday Times* by then."

"So you were working for MI6 too?"

"I wouldn't put it as strongly as that. Just the odd job here and there, filling out someone's cover, that sort of thing."

"As with Fleming?"

"Yes, a journalist doing a feature on post-war Italian tourism, with his wife and child in tow. And it all worked out very well. One of Dylan's regular visitors in Florence was Luigi Berti. He lived on Elba and was Italy's leading expert on English literature. It couldn't have been better! As soon as Dylan said he'd like to visit the island, Berti arranged everything. Then we got the British Council to place a few stories on Dylan in the local papers. Britain's leading socialist poet, that sort of thing, who'd opposed the Mosleyites in the Swansea Plaza.

"So when Dylan and family arrived in Rio Marina, they were met by the Mayor and the town band. Lots of speeches and spumante, flowers for the children. Berti had found them lodgings with his cousin Giovanni who ran the Albergo Elba, overlooking the fruit market. Fleming and I arrived a few days later. We stayed in the Clara, on Via Palestro, next to the port, which was perfect.

"Dylan spent the time wandering round the town, just like he did at New Quay. You couldn't miss him in his pink shirt and green trousers. He used to sit on a rock in the harbour reading the thrillers that Margaret Taylor had sent him, and when he'd finished he just threw them into the sea. Sometimes we took a picnic and walked along the cliff from the watch tower to the little bay at Porticciolo. It was magical!

"Fleming's job was to keep an eye on the ore being loaded on the ships and check it against the official dockets. These were smuggled in every day by Marco Gravelli, the quarry manager, who was actually working for the Italian security service. In the evenings, Fleming had to make contact with the workers, and that was where Dylan came in, of course. By now, he knew everybody in the cafés around the port.

"Everything went well until the day before we were supposed to leave. Brigit had already gone back to Florence with the children. Caitlin and Fleming were out dancing somewhere. Dylan, Waldo and I went out for dinner and ended up in the Bar Karl Marx, just off the Via Pascole. The bar's still there. It's a mecca for the old-guard communists. There's even a photograph of Harry Pollitt addressing the Durham Miners Gala. His daughter married someone from Elba, you know, a pastry cook from Lacona.

"Anyway, Dylan was talking about going home, moaning about having to live in Oxford again. These men came in, miners. They grabbed Dylan and shouted 'Churchill spy!' Wrong Prime Minister but we got the message. They took us outside and bundled us into the back of an old American jeep. Gravelli the manager was in there, too, badly beaten up, and shackled to the seat.

"We were driven out past the Appiano tower into the hills. I really wasn't aware of very much. I was worried stiff for Waldo. Dylan was sitting quietly, looking very gloomy. Doing a bit on the side for MI6 must have seemed very glamorous to him, and well paid, but this was a different matter. We must have travelled for about an hour up a mountain track when the jeep stopped. Gravelli was unshackled and pushed out onto the ground. I could hear them dragging him through the bushes. There was a terrible scream and then a gunshot. The men got back into the car, and we carried on up the mountain.

"Eventually, we stopped again. They pushed us out, and told us to start walking along this tiny sheep track. I thought the end had come. Waldo was crying, more from hunger than anything else. We came out into a clearing, a kind of quarry I thought, where there was another man waiting for us, not Italian going by his looks, and he seemed to take charge. They marched us over to an old stone building. Luigi Berti was inside. We sat round a table. Berti passed some bottles of beer to Dylan. 'You English people... your wife sleeps with Giovanni, and also goes dancing with Signor Fleming. You go out to dinner with Signora Fleming and her baby. We watch you. You are old friends. The baby has your nose...'

"'The English bond very quickly in foreign parts.'

"'I was very muffed to be deceived,' said Berti. 'I asked these people to welcome you.'

"'Miffed,' replied Dylan.

"'There are no pedants in the graveyard, signor.'

"'Why have we been brought here?'

"'They say you are a spy not a poet.'

"Dylan opened the bottle with his teeth, spat the cap onto the table and said: 'I'm Dylan Thomas from Swansea, my father was a coal miner who wore a white muffler and was miffed that he couldn't write poetry but I most certainly do, boyo. And what's more,' he said, puffing out his chest like a bull frog, 'I'm a member of the National Liberal Club'.

"Berti shrugged his shoulders. 'Dylan Thomas is a poet, a very good one, but are you him?' He reached into his bag and took out a newspaper clipping. It was the *South Wales Evening Post*. 'Look, you are Signor Daniel Jones, composer and Bletchley Park spy, and moonlighting – is that your expression? – with MI6. This man here in the other photograph is Dylan Thomas.'

"'They've got the bloody captions wrong,' screamed Dylan. And they had. The *Post* had run a story on the Kardomah Boys and had mixed up Dan and Dylan. Not the first time it had happened.

"Berti passed some sheets of paper across to Dylan. 'Write,' he said. 'Show me proof.'

"Dylan looked furious. 'I cannot and I will not write to order.'

"'Either that or you both join Signor Gravelli'.

"'And the baby will go to the orphanage'. This was the new man speaking for the first time. Almost faultless English but not quite.

"Dylan got up and stamped around the table. 'I'll need more beer and cigarettes. Food for the baby. And these boys out of here.' I was amazed at how cool he was. I was shaking all over. I wasn't sure that Dylan could write poetry any more. He hadn't written anything for more than two years, not since he'd been in New Quay. And remember, Berti was no fool. He knew his English literature, he'd translated Henry James and Virginia Woolf.

"Dylan wrote until the sun came up. Berti sent for coffee and panini, took the sheets of paper from Dylan and started to read. The tension in the room was awful. Our lives depended on Dylan's words, it was a kind of literary Russian roulette.

"Berti read the first page in complete silence, but then he started to chuckle. Dylan winked at me, and picked up Waldo to give him some breakfast. For the first time, I felt things were going our way. Then Berti called in the men from the other room. 'Grappa, please, for a great poet.' And he came across and shook Dylan's hand, and gave me a kiss on the cheek. 'This will make Dylan Thomas a famous man'.

"When the men were seated, Berti started to read:

"'To begin with the beginning... *Per cominciare dal principio*

"'It is a summer, moonless night in the small sea town of Elohesra, starless and coal black, the cobbled streets silent, and the crouched, chestnut woods toppling invisible down to the slow black, low-backed, black as a bible sea.

"'*Notte d'estate illune e senza stelle, nera come il carbone, nella cittadina di mare de Elohesra, silenziose le vie acciottolate, e un bosco di castagni accovacciato si getta invisibile nel lento, indolente nero, dal dorso basso, mare di color Bibbia.*'

"And so it went on. The miners loved every word. When Berti finished, there was a loud round of applause, and more grappa. Berti turned to Dylan: 'This Elohesra with its milky wood and little harbour, this is a Paradise, no? A Miltonian allusion, I think.'

"'Oh, no,' said Dylan quickly. 'It's Rio Marina.' That seemed to make everyone even more happy. Then there was a silly argument about which of the town's quarries Signor Waldo and Signorina Garter made love in. Of course, it wasn't the whole of

Milk Wood, just the first twenty pages or so. The men were amazed that Dylan had only been in Rio a fortnight yet knew all the goings-on in the town. They couldn't believe he knew about Signor Verni the tailor up on Via Pini and Signorina Luzi of the gelateria, who sent love letters to each other every day but could not marry because her father was a Stalinist, and he hated Signor Verni for making suits for Trotsky.

"And that was that. We were back in Rio for lunch and caught the ferry to the mainland."

"And Caitlin and Fleming?" I asked.

"Fleming was far more resourceful, as you might expect," replied Rosalind. "He and Caitlin swam out into the harbour, stole a fishing boat and got away to Piombino."

"So *Milk Wood* started on Elba?"

"In a way, but it had been in Dylan's head since New Quay." Rosalind paused and called Leno Conti across to pay the bill. "You should visit Rio Marina some day. Waldo goes back every year. It's just like it says in *Milk Wood*, the little town beneath the wooded slopes, the harbour, the quarries, the fishermen. And Rio's postman did actually open the letters. He was the official censor for the Party on the island."

"What happened to those twenty pages of script?"

"They're in the Museo dei Minerali, on the Piazza d'Acquisto."

"Let me pay the bill."

"*Ah, Leno, i ricciarelli erano squisiti.*"

"*Questa, cara signora, e una bellisima storia.*"

"And Marco Gravelli?" I asked.

"We were caught between a rock and a hard place. We said nothing, though I believe Fleming reported the matter when he returned. But they were not times for justice."

"Only of the roughest kind."

"Count your blessings, Martin. We got *Milk Wood*. Read Dylan's letters. He loved Elba. A world by itself, he said. Happiness in a world that never was. More important, Caitlin was happy. She had the sun, the dancing, the swimming, the good food and Brigit to look after the children. And Giovanni, of course. *Milk Wood* was born in Caitlin's smile that summer."

We got up to leave. "By the way," I said, escorting her to the door. "We noticed there aren't any letters from Dylan before May 1949."

Rosalind looked flushed and confused. "We probably saw too much of each to bother writing," she replied unconvincingly.

"There's not even a post card from Italy. He was there five months. You'd have thought he'd have written."

"They probably got lost in the post," she said, and walked off down the High Street.

★ ★ ★

I remember the morning was glim – Rachel's word for a grey day when the clouds were settled on the tree tops, and the drabness squeezed so much energy from you it was barely possible to make a cup of tea or answer the phone. White sky depression it's called here, and it especially blights the lives of incomers who've usually seen Wales only in summer sunshine as they make their decision to buy a house and move here.

Half way through the desultory morning, we forced ourselves to go outside and potter in the garden. Rachel began clearing the asparagus bed and I walked down to the small meadow that lay between the vegetable garden and the river. It was regularly flooded so growing vegetables was out of the question. But we'd planted two rows of willows to make a tunnel that ran from the gate down to Rachel's poetry hut. I had a roll of string and some scissors and my intention was to tie in some of the bigger willows before they grew away from me.

The Aeron was full and swirling brown with silt from the hills. Along the banks were large mounds of creamy foam caused by chemicals leached out of the conifer plantations by heavy rainfall the night before. They bobbed up and down on the waves of the river as if children had thrown candy floss from the bridge. A swollen river also brought its share of swimming sheep, and a good number that were already drowned. These were swept downstream to the sea on the full tide, beaching on the stony shore to be scooped up by yellow-gaitered workmen from the Council.

Some sheep never made it to the sea, but were trapped by swooping branches or caught between boulders that came out like black snares from the bed of the river. There they might stay for weeks, stenching the air as magpies and rooks feasted through the carcass, till nothing was left but a frame of bones to bleach in the sun and slip gradually down to settle on the stones of the riverbed. It was best to remove these sheep before the feasting began, to push them out into mid-stream, where they would carry on down river for the Council to deal with.

I'd been working on the willow tunnel for about hour. Rachel poured some tea from the thermos, and while it cooled, I wandered aimlessly upstream hoping to catch a glimpse of something exotic, a kingfisher or the pair of escaped parrots that had made their home in the roof of an old stable on the other bank. I stopped near our only oak tree, patted its trunk and looked upstream to the bridge. There was a sheep caught on a branch that hung low in the Aeron. I could see a large rook sitting on its neck, pecking at the back of its head.

I returned to the garden, found my long-handled spade and walked back up the bank. As I got closer, I could see that the rook's beak was deep in the sheep's skull, and so engrossed that I had to clap my hands to persuade it to fly away. I was distracted by the noise of a tractor stopping on the bridge, then the sound of men's voices. When I looked back at the sheep I realised it was a man face down in the river. I half-recognised the Arran sweater and knew instinctively this was Ogmore Stillness.

I called to the farmers on the bridge, who ran down the slope into the field. We hauled the body from the river and laid the man on the bank. Leeches clung to his bloated face, and more huddled together in the folds of his neck. We stared nervously at him but Ogmore Stillness could not stare back. His eyelids had been stitched together with rose thorns. Nor could he hear the river washing by or the wind in the trees, for someone had sliced off his ears.

Rachel had run back to the house and phoned for the police. A car arrived within minutes. I took the constables across the field, showed them the corpse and left them to it. The lane was soon blocked to traffic, as more police vehicles and an ambulance arrived. Two officers were climbing into their wet suits on our lawn, holding onto the flowering cherry for support as they hopped from one leg to the other. Some of their colleagues struggled to carry a large canvas tent across the muddy field, complaining loudly about the state of their boots. Locals were arriving, lured by the sirens and numbed quiet by the awesome prospect of a big event in the village. All this we watched from our back room that looked down across the field to the river.

Some time later, I was interviewed by an Inspector from Aberystwyth. I told him that I had met Stillness in the pub some days ago, that he was with his family renting a cottage nearby, and that they had been looking at properties in the area, including Fern Hill. He asked me who else had been in the pub, and I told him. He informed me that a long-handled spade had been found on the bank near the floating body. Did I know whose it was? It was mine, I replied, and he said that it would be taken away for examination, bearing in mind the nature of the injury to the deceased's head. I was too bewildered to take in the implication fully.

We stood at the window for the next hour or so, watching the comings and goings in the field. Gradually, the crowd of sightseers on the bridge dwindled to a little boy and his grandfather.

We took the car, drove to the coast and walked across the sands to New Quay. We had a late lunch and afterwards walked along the cliffs. Most of this we did in silence. A cold evening wind forced us inland, and we returned to the car through narrow country lanes. We were exhausted but we had walked the shock out of our systems.

★ ★ ★

On Sunday, Rachel went to her Quaker Meeting and I walked up to the Post Office for the papers. I was surprised at how little interest was shown in the murder. I suspected that the village would have been more affected if the body had been found on dry land. That would have meant the killer was probably a local person. But Stillness could have been killed anywhere upstream, more likely, said some, in the rough spots of Talsarn where things could get very boisterous on a Friday night.

Rachel arrived back just before lunch. Usually she returns from Meeting in a tranquil or elated state, the effect of sitting in silent worship for an hour, or of particularly uplifting ministry from one of the group. She was always buoyed by the support she found in the closeness of the circle. Occasionally she came home angry, but never did she come home looking, as she did now, as if she had been to the dentist. She was pale, and looked troubled.

I scrambled some eggs with tarragon and bacon bits chopped in, and we sat in silence around the small white table in the garden room. I made a pot of tea, and then another. I washed up, still waiting for the moment. I dried the dishes. I put them away. I cleaned the kitchen counters. I swept the floor. As I rounded the corner into the passage-way, the broom brushed up against her feet. She was leaning against the doorpost, her arms folded, looking at the floor. I sensed the time was right and said: "Well?"

"We were in Lampeter today."

I nodded. Quakers don't have churches, they have Meeting Houses. But Rachel's Meeting was peripatetic and twice a month they met in the library in the Philosophy Department. On the other Sundays, it was held in the sitting room of a remote farm-house up in the hills, where the only philosopher on offer was a barn owl who usually sat for the entire Meeting on a bird table outside the window.

"I was on the door, welcoming people in, and on the look-out for any newcomers. There were seven people already in the room, and I didn't really expect any more. I was about to go in, when the front door opened and a gust of wind blew down the passage, blowing the papers off the table. I waited but nobody came. I walked back up towards the front door, and there was a man there, sitting on the canvas chair, shaking and trembling as if he were freezing to death. 'Have you come to Meeting?' I asked. He nodded, without looking up. 'I'll show you the way,' I said, and cupped his elbow with my hand. He got up and walked beside me down the passage. 'Have you been to Meeting before?' He shook his head. I gave him that little leaflet on Quaker Worship that we give to newcomers, and he stuffed it in his pocket. We reached the door and I said: 'Come on in.' We stepped inside. 'I'm Rachel, by the way.' And then he looked up. That was the first time I'd seen his face. 'Waldo Hilton,' he replied, and he walked across the room to the far side of the circle and sat next to Dot.

"Now it was my turn to shake, my legs were so wobbly I could hardly get to my seat. No, I know what you're going to ask, but I just couldn't tell whether he was the man who killed Mably. I was terribly twitchy and agitated but then somebody stood up and did this nice little ministry about finding a well, and how he tried to get it going again, and all the foul, black stuff that poured out of the tap for a week and then suddenly the waters ran clear. That made me think of Dylan. I looked at Waldo and he was crying, and Dot was holding his hand to comfort him. Somehow, that settled me for the rest of the Meeting, though I wasn't completely calm because I felt as if Waldo was staring at me, but when I opened my eyes and looked across at him, he was looking at the ground, and sobbing still. I can't explain it. Anyway, we all shook hands at the end of the hour, as usual. I saw Dot talking to Waldo, and then he disappeared."

"What did he say to her?"

"I'm here slinking from my mousehole."

"That must have fazed her."

"It's from Dylan's poem, 'Lament'," explained Rachel. She reached for *Collected Poems*, and opened it for me to read. "It's about sex," I eventually said, not noticing Rachel's withering look. "It's about Dylan's declining sexual prowess."

"He's only using sex as a symbol, to lament the ascendancy of body and flesh, of earthly things, of matter over spirit. Look at the last stanza, there's so much joy there, something's happened, someone's helped him to crawl out of the mousehole."

"Merle?"

"Merle as Quaker. Dylan found something special in the Meetings, a new inner experience, his soul found a sabbath wife, as he puts it, he pushed the beast behind him and saw an angel."

"A lament for not finding God's love before?"

"Precisely." Rachel gave me another disparaging look and said: "No woman would think 'Lament' was about sex."

I slunk back to my mousehole, sniffed around and came up with another question of more immediate importance. "And what's Waldo up to, coming to Meeting? Has he seen the light, like his dad?"

"Either that or he's trying to intimidate me."

"Perhaps it's time I had another chat with Rosalind."

★ ★ ★

I invited Rosalind to lunch at the Scadan Coch the next day. She arrived early, dressed in a white blouse and jeans, and wearing sunglasses. She looked more like fifty than eighty as she came through the door. The pub was already filling up. It was the start of the Ciliau Poetry Fest which O'Malley organised each year. Despite the quality of the poetry, I suspected that most people came for O'Malley's cooking, because on each day of the Fest he prepared menus inspired by Eliot's or Dylan's poems.

We sat at the Wordsworth table and read the menu. Rosalind dithered over Surprise of Sweeney Erect and Tagine Burnt Norton, eventually choosing the latter, a pot of lamb, apricots and rice, cooked long and slow with garlic and onions until a thick, black crust formed on the bottom. I went for Salad of Long-Legged Bait – scallops and cockles in a white wine sauce, vine leaves stuffed with laverbread and shallots, with mozzarella and chopped tomatoes on the side. I skipped the Brains and joined Rosalind in a bottle of Mumbles Pomeroy which O'Malley commissioned each year for the Fest. We made small talk. I didn't quite know the tactful way of saying: 'Your son may have killed my dog and Ogmore Stillness, and is trying to frighten my wife.' So I said: "I hear Waldo's selling the farm."

And she said: "I hear you found Ogmore Stillness' body."

"You sound as if you knew him."

"Not exactly."

"I met him here in the pub last week. He was off to view Fern Hill."

"The police have questioned Waldo, and the people in the other properties that Stillness visited, including me."

I think my mouth dropped open, or the fork fell out of my hand, but Rosalind certainly had a look of triumph on her face. "You know more about this than I do," I said.

"After his visits, Stillness had a phone call to go back to London."

"That's where his wife assumed he was, while all the time he was floating in the Aeron," said O'Malley as he put the food on the table. "And it wasn't robbery. His wallet and car keys were still in his trousers."

There was no point in asking them how they knew all this. They were on the village intranet. As a newcomer, I wasn't.

"They were trying to buy a cottage down here," I volunteered, as if this would astonish them, but it was the best I could do.

"No, they weren't," said O'Malley.

"He was thieving," added Rosalind.

"Not money, mind, just our literary heritage."

I gave up. "You'd better explain."

"Dylan's not just a poet any more, he's an icon."

"No, I mean explain, as in start from the beginning."

"They sell bits of his bow-ties for hundreds of dollars."

"A single letter to Caitlin would fetch £6,000 at auction," added O'Malley, sitting down beside us.

"And it was probably Ogmore Stillness who stole the shed. Worth a fortune in America."

I looked at them both in desperation. O'Malley got up, filled our glasses, and went behind the bar. "Rosalind," I said quietly, "I think you'll have to take this one step at a time."

"Ogmore Stillness visited me, Fern Hill, Talsarn, New Quay."

I saw some light. "He's a Dylan Thomas buff?"

"No, he's a literary scavenger."

"He's a collector?"

"No, he works for an auctioneer specialising in writers' memorabilia."

"So he wasn't buying cottages?"

"No, that's just one of the covers he uses."

"What happened at Waldo's?"

"Waldo came back from the fields and found him inside the house. Stillness seemed unperturbed, said he'd heard the farm was for sale. Waldo threatened to call the police. Stillness took out a bundle of twenty pound notes. 'Just the first instalment, old boy', was what he said. 'Your mother wants you to sell me Dylan's papers.'

"When Waldo said 'no', Stillness offered to introduce him to a newspaper reporter so that he could tell the world about Dylan and his love child. 'They'll pay you a fortune, old chap.' Waldo saw the blackmail and threw him out into the yard. Then he noticed the photograph of Dylan was missing. He chased after Stillness and asked for it back. Stillness swung a fist, Waldo brought him to the ground and found the photograph in his coat pocket. End of visit."

"And then Stillness came to see you?"

"Yes, but his manner was rather different. He was very polite, even charming. He claimed he represented a firm specialising in literary acquisitions. It was common knowledge, he said, that Dylan and I had been intimate friends. He wondered if there were letters and papers that survived? His interest was purely to cast new light on Dylan's character so that the image of the 'drunken bohemian poet', as he put it, could be laid to rest. His firm were prepared to showcase Dylan in London and New York and pay for serious academic study of any new material.

"I told him that all of Dylan's papers were being prepared for publication – I didn't mention Rachel by name."

"And who killed Stillness and why?"

"I'd rather not speculate – let's leave that to our clever policemen."

O'Malley appeared from the kitchen carrying a large plate. "Milk Wood Gateau," he said, putting it on the table between us. "Laced with *poteen*. Enjoy."

I cut the cake and gave us both a slice. I wanted to get back to Waldo: "He attended Rachel's Meeting yesterday."

"I know. He came to see me last night, so I wasn't surprised when you suggested lunch today."

"But why Rachel's Meeting?"

"It's fifty years since Dylan first went to Meeting with Merle in New York."

"I don't understand."

"Waldo's life is not his own. Not just the voices, but he can't get away from Dylan. He can't help it but he finds himself doing things that Dylan did. A few years ago, he went to Czech classes and filled the house with travel brochures, though in the end he didn't actually go to Prague. It's the anniversaries of significant moments in Dylan's life that affect him the most, he seems to act out what Dylan did, though I'm sure he doesn't understand that he's doing it."

I thought immediately of the anniversary of the shooting at Majoda. "What happened in 1995?"

"I dreaded the year from its very beginning but it turned out wonderfully. Waldo excelled himself."

"No shoot-outs at the bungalow?"

"No, a charity event for Mencap." Rosalind had a gift for surprise.

"Go on, tell me."

"Waldo organised a sponsored ride from Talsarn to New Quay, passing all the places that Dylan knew. He borrowed a pony, and covered it with a white sheet, so that all you could see was the head and tail, and four little brown feet sticking out at the bottom. O'Malley embroidered the edges with a thin red line, broken up by clumps of daffodils. On the sides of the sheet, he put scenes from Dylan's life, not just local, but skyscrapers for New York, oil wells for Iran, the leaning tower of Pisa, that sort of thing. On the pony's rear was the bungalow at Majoda, with a man standing outside in a balaclava helmet, holding a machine gun. Not historically accurate, the balaclava, but O'Malley had seen too much footage from Belfast."

"What happened to the sheet?"

"You sound like Ogmore Stillness."

"It sounds like a work of art, and it's not here in the pub."

"It was auctioned for Mencap."

"Who bought it?"

"A young woman from Bethlehem," she replied, making it clear with her eyes that she wanted no more interruptions. "Waldo decorated the pony with various objects – a spanner for Dylan, a mauve Isodora Duncan scarf draped around the neck of the pony for Caitlin. And a *menorah* for me, tied elegantly to the pony's tail with blue ribbon."

"For Eliot?"

"An air raid warden's hat. Then there were three teddy bears, one each for Dylan's other children, Waldo's half-siblings, of course."

Rosalind paused whilst O'Malley cleared away the empty plates. "We set off in stately procession from Talsarn, after a blessing from the vicar, and a reading by Waldo of 'Love in the Asylum'. I must say, Waldo looked magnificent. He'd been down to Laugharne, and borrowed an old robe from the Portreeve's office, a deep brown velvet edged in white fur, with golden stars running down the sleeves to the cuffs. On his head, he put a tricorne, symbolising the sea that Dylan loved so much, as did Eliot, of course. We followed the Aeron..."

"We?"

"Waldo and me, people from the village like O'Malley, the children from the school who'd been given the morning off, and people joined in as we walked along. It was a glorious frosty morning. The river was sparkling and bubbly, and the sun shone warm on our backs. Now and again a patch of river mist would swallow us up, and we'd shiver with the cold until we were through into the sun again, with Waldo leading us out, waving his tricorne, and reciting chunks of Dylan's poetry off by heart. And all around, the trees, shivering bare, looking in the mist like another thousand people cheering us on.

"The children skipped along behind the pony. The girls had kazoos and tambourines, and the boys had made drums from old tin cans. A fox followed us on the far bank, a hungry, blazing, dog fox, who came along behind, keeping a respectful distance, but stopping and watching, sniffing at the air, and ever so curious about what was happening, and he stayed with us all the way to the Beech Walk. A group of women were waiting for us, and they pinned little sprays of rosemary to the sheet, and then Waldo danced along the path with them. And every time we stopped, Waldo would take out a little silver cup from his pocket, sip some brandy, and throw the rest to the ground.

"We eventually arrived at Tyglyn Aeron for lunch where Waldo read 'To Others than You' and then bits from 'The Waste Land'. Afterwards, the children went back to Talsarn and the rest of us walked along the old railway line to Aberaeron, and stayed the night in the Feathers as a birthday treat. The next day we set off along the coast path to New Quay. That was magical, too, because the dolphins were out and they stayed with us all along the coast. The gorse was yellow on the cliff tops, and the air smelt of coconut and seaweed. There were peregrines about, swooping on the sea gulls, and we even saw a pair of choughs. There was a wonderful brightness in Waldo's eyes that I hadn't seen for ages. The year had started well for him, he'd been completely free of his voices, and now, on his birthday, he seemed so joyful.

"We pulled up outside Majoda. Waldo read 'The conversation of prayers', and made a little speech. He said we should always remember great men for what they might have done, not for what they actually did but he broke down in tears, and didn't finish. He toasted Dylan's memory with the last drop of brandy. We raffled all the objects on the pony, including the sheet as I mentioned, but not the spanner because that was Waldo's special thing for killing the geese at Christmas. It had actually been stolen by Dylan from the boot of Howard de Walden's sports car. It was a collector's piece in its own right but it was doubly valuable because Dylan had used it to take the tops off his Buckleys."

"And yesterday, it was the same?" I asked, not disguising the note of scepticism in my voice. I knew by now how skilled Rosalind was in taking me away from the issue I wanted to explore. "An anniversary, the first Quaker Meeting with Merle?"

"I think so."

"Dylan went to Meeting because he was in love with Merle." Rosalind looked shocked. "What are you suggesting?"

"I'm worried that Waldo is fixating on Rachel."

"That's ridiculous. His voices are quiet – Butcher Beynon has let him be."

"And Pugh the Poisoner?"

★ ★ ★

As a sociologist, I could put together some of what was happening for myself. Merle was Jewish and, according to Dylan's first letter to Rosalind, a converted Quaker. So was Rachel. Dylan had been in love with Merle, and now Waldo was building a relationship with Rachel. The next layer was that Waldo's mother, Rosalind, also Jewish, had been Dylan's lover. Around the twin maypoles of Waldo and Dylan, spun a blurring, conflated image of three Jewish women.

Psycho-babble, perhaps, but something was unfolding that I sensed put Rachel in danger, and I had no doubt that all this was somehow related to the murder of Ogmore Stillness. Perhaps it was something simple: did Waldo see Ogmore Stillness and Rachel as literary scavengers, each gaining in their own different way from picking over Dylan's bones? It was possible that Waldo resented anything that might unpick his fragile, but carefully constructed, sense of self-hood. Perhaps Waldo wanted us to know Dylan only as we presently know him, because this was the Dylan upon whom Waldo's own identity had been built.

Never mind the half-baked analysis, Rachel would say, try a bit of TLC. If Waldo continued to come to Meeting, she would see this as an opportunity to offer help and support to someone ill. This was how the others would see it, too. They understood how the Meeting could be therapeutic and empowering. Indeed, many of them, including Rachel, had themselves been helped through various personal crises by the opportunity the Meeting gave, particularly in its silence, for stocktaking and insight. They would not be deterred by Waldo's eccentricities.

I realised I would need more convincing arguments if I were to persuade Rachel so I rang an old friend and sometime Professor of Psychiatry, Cressida Lovewhich. She was not at home.

I first met Cressida in the cells of Paddington police station in 1968, after being arrested at a Vietnam war demonstration. I had found myself, quite by chance, amongst the first ranks of demonstrators pushing up against the police outside the American Embassy. We were in the front line but our behaviour was largely determined by the thousands behind. As they surged forward, a wave of energy would crash through the crowd, sweeping those in front against the police cordon. During a lull between waves, I saw a young woman lying on the open ground behind the police. Blood flowed from a wound to her head. I asked the policemen in front of me if I could help her, and, to my surprise, they let me through. I was naive in those days, and thought they were being considerate. I knelt down beside the woman. Her head wound wasn't as bad as it had looked, and she seemed more shaken than hurt. I was reaching into my pocket for a handkerchief, when I felt an immense blow across my upper arm. I looked up at three policemen around me with truncheons drawn. I leapt to my feet and covered my head as they rained blows on my shoulders and back. I was taken to the police bus and, when it was full, we were driven off to Paddington police station where I was put in a large cell with about twenty others. About half an hour later, the cell door opened, and a small group of women demonstrators was thrown in. The woman whom I'd gone to help sat beside me. We were there together for several hours, and got on like a house on fire. She was Cressida, an art history student, and the daughter of a baron; I was a sociologist writing a thesis on the British peerage, and the son of a bankrupt alcoholic. We talked and held hands, more in comradeship than anything else, because we also discovered that we were both members of the International Socialists. Of such things, lifelong friendships are formed.

At about seven o'clock, an extremely large and muscular policeman entered the cell and escorted me out. "I'm PC Softwell," he said, "and you're being done for assaulting me." I was charged and fingerprinted and asked if I wanted to make a phone call. I rang home and asked my father to stand bail for £15. Certainly not, he replied, if you're daft enough to hit an officer of the law then you deserve all you get. I heard my stepmother belching in the background and put down the phone. I was returned to the cell. A little later, Cressida was taken out. When she came back she said that her mother had agreed to bail us both. We were released about an hour later. "Mummy's gone," said Cressida, "but she's left Bissmire."

We went outside where the air smelt like Bonfire Night, for demonstrators from Germany had bought fireworks to throw under the hooves of the police horses. A chauffeur waited for us beside a silver Rolls Royce. We turned round, raised our clenched fists at the blue lamp, and climbed into the car. "Ronnie Scott's," said Cressida to Bissmire. I opened the drinks cabinet. Cressida drew the curtains across the dividing window and began to unbutton her blouse. That was the first and only time we made love in a friendship that has lasted thirty years.

The following day I bought *The Guardian* and, on the front page, was a photograph of me being beaten by the three policemen, with two others advancing to help. The photographer was someone I had known before when I worked in the school holidays as a copy boy on the *Evening Post*.

I appeared at the magistrates court on the Marylebone Road. My solicitor entered *The Guardian* photograph in evidence, and the photographer testified that he had taken it. He presented enlargements of the photograph which showed the identity numbers of the policemen arresting me. None of them was PC Softwell. How did PC Softwell account for that? asked my solicitor. He couldn't. I was still found guilty and fined £25. Cressida paid, and afterwards we went to lunch at Maurer's.

Within a year, Cressida moved from art history to art therapy to a psychology degree, and was expelled from the International Socialists for declaring that Marx might have developed a better analysis if he had been able to read Freud first. She joined the Communist Party, met Vauby Preston, a child psychiatrist, and I was their best man when they were 'married' in a humanist ceremony in the tenants' hall on Woodberry Down estate. Her parents were invited, but declined to come. Cressida took a job as a social worker, then became a lecturer in applied psychology at the South Bank Poly, and eventually was appointed to a Chair of Psychiatry in London University. In the meantime, Vauby had joined the Tavistock Institute, and became the director of the child support unit. In 1988, they resigned their posts and joined an aid agency setting up psychiatric reconstruction camps to counsel those traumatised by civil war. They worked first in Angola, and then they were asked to go to Rwanda. In their third week, their jeep went over a land mine. Vauby was killed instantly. Cressida received severe chest and face injuries.

I wondered why she was not at home. I desperately needed to talk to her about Waldo. I rang her aid agency. She was, they told me, on a new tour of duty in Yugoslavia. She was expected back in a month or so.

It was to be a tense and difficult month. Waldo continued to attend Rachel's Sunday Meeting. He became more relaxed and out-going. Rachel noticed he smiled more, and was able to keep eye-contact with people when he talked with them. He listened attentively to any ministry that was offered, and always stayed behind to help with washing the coffee cups: "My dad couldn't take the top off an egg," he said, the first time he offered to help. He asked about books he could read that would tell him more about the persecution of Quakers in Wales. On the third Sunday, he arrived with a bowl of plastic flowers to put on the table that stood inside the circle where people sat. Rosalind confirmed that "Waldo's feeling hugely better. He says his head's emptying." Rachel interpreted this positively, that the influence of his voices was abating as a result of coming to Meeting.

Then out of the blue Cressida Lovewhich telephoned. We talked a little about Yugoslavia, and then I told her everything I knew about Waldo, and my worries. She said she would ring back after she'd had time to think about it. About a week, she said. Later, I e-mailed her the notes I had made of my conversations with Rosalind.

And what a week. On Tuesday, the police made an appointment to see me. I spent two days as nervous as a dancing duck but they only wanted to return my long-handled spade, which had been eliminated from their enquiries.

On Thursday, Waldo turned up, unasked and uninvited, to the launch of Rachel's second collection of poems. We'd invited friends to lunch in the village hall. Rachel's parents came down from London, bringing salt beef, gefilte fish, spiced carp and a boxful of bagels and onion platzels. Other guests brought food, too, and we provided the wine. I noticed Waldo slipping in just before Rachel started reading some of her poems. Of course, she was delighted to see him, as were the others from her Meeting, but I was angry. It felt like an intrusion. What was worse, he spent the whole time taking photographs of Rachel. Not just during the readings, but whatever she did, wherever she went, inside or out.

Cressida phoned on Friday morning. "I've been taking this seriously," she began, "because someone's been murdered. How often does that happen in your village? What was the motive? Not robbery. Was he murdered because he was an obnoxious Englishman?"

"Most unlikely," though, as I said that, I thought of O'Malley.

That's what a murder does in a small community – it makes you think the worst of the most unlikely people.

"A random, chance killing in the countryside?"

"I wouldn't have thought so."

"Now look at Waldo. Here's a man with a mental health problem. And he's the only one in the whole story who has a connection to Stillness. Did you tell the police about that?"

"No."

"Isn't that odd?"

"It would be a breach of Rosalind's trust. Everything I know about Waldo has come through her."

"You're afraid to tell the police in case Rosalind takes back Dylan's papers from Rachel."

"It's not enough to go to the police with, not enough to break someone's trust."

"What if somebody else is killed?"

I recalled the seminars I taught on the ethics of sociology. Should the researcher respect the anonymity of his informants in all circumstances? Was there any difference between the sociologist and the priest in the confessional? Wasn't the sociologist (and especially one turned private detective) entitled, like the journalist, to protect his sources?

"You could be seen as withholding evidence."

"I'm withholding conjecture."

"So what do you want from me?"

"An understanding of Waldo."

Cressida sighed with exasperation. "Not a definitive analysis," I continued, "just a few pointers."

"Whatever's wrong with Waldo," she replied, "he's going through it on his own – didn't you say his wife made off with the fertiliser rep?"

"She did, but I don't think Waldo was ever married to her."

* * *

On Sunday, Rachel came back from Meeting and told me that

Waldo hadn't turned up. Quakers always notice when someone doesn't come to Meeting, partly because numbers are small so it's obvious who's sitting in the circle and who's not. But Quakers are also good at cherishing others. It's even in their Rules and Regs – "Remember that each one of us is unique, precious, a child of God."

After lunch, at which we talked mostly about Waldo, we went to our local animal sanctuary, which had phoned us to say they had a young collie for sale. We drove out through the village, and turned onto a stony track that led down into a hidden, wooded valley. As we reached the bottom, cats and kittens came rolling out of the long grass onto the track in front of us, like circus tumblers. On our left was a field of chickens and ducks, and beyond it, one with donkeys and ponies. To the right, a ploughed morass of mud, home to a group of black pygmy pigs abandoned, so local gossip told us, by a discontented wife who'd been given them by her husband as a present on their wedding anniversary.

We pulled into the yard. A tall, red-haired woman in patched jeans, and an over-sized sweater almost to her knees, came striding across, hand out-stretched. I wondered if she raided her own charity clothes bags. "Let's go inside," she said, opening the door into an old mill house. We went into a circular room, with white-washed walls and honey-brown beams. On the chimney breast hung a huge mosaic triptych, like the stained glass panels of a church window. "Cleo Mussi," she said in explanation as she saw Rachel looking in admiration. "Made from broken cups and saucers." We crossed to the kitchen at the side of the house. A black and white collie came skidding across the granite floor, its tail in extravagant semaphore, burying its teeth into Rachel's boots. "Meet Bedwen. Welsh for birch tree." The pup raised its white-socked paw in greeting. "The only one of five to survive. The whole litter put in a sack and thrown in the river. I'm sure you'll be happy with her."

"Can we look around?" Rachel was a sucker for animals. She carried a trowel in the back of the car. Every time we came across a squashed animal, she'd stop the car, scoop the remains off the road, and take it home to give it a decent burial. It often took us a long time to get anywhere.

"There's a jumble sale at three, so I'll leave you to yourselves."

We wandered around the animal pens, with Bedwen pulling on the lead as if she wanted to get away as quickly as possible. Rachel became engaged in a discussion with one of the volunteers about whether it would be kinder to put dogs down rather than keep them for months on end locked up in their little cages. I edged off towards the square of trestle tables that had been set up for the jumble sale. I bought some raspberry jam and a bottle of elderflower champagne, and then found myself at a table piled high with books. I became immensely irritated because no-one had sorted them into useful categories. I looked round for Rachel but she was nowhere to be seen, probably buying a one-eyed, broken-backed cat to take home with us. So I tied Bedwen to the table leg, and set to, sorting the paperbacks from the hard backs, and then gradually working out the best categories for the paperbacks. I'd just finished sorting the fiction into various genres when Rachel appeared, thankfully without cat or any other creature. She flipped through the poetry pile and said: "There's more than a dozen books here by Eliot, or about him."

I went across to the jumble organiser and asked her if she remembered who'd brought the Eliot books. She said that they'd been left in a plastic bag outside the gate a week or so ago. Had there been anything else in the bag? Odds and ends, including a malacca cane, back copies of *Boxing News*, and a spanner. I found the cane and the spanner on the bric-a-brac stall. I unscrewed the top of the cane. There was a discoloured tooth inside. The spanner was heavy and beautiful. The steel handle was inlaid with brass art deco designs, and the head had been curved to suggest the arching neck of a dragon. I paid five pounds for the cane and a tenner for the spanner.

"The murder weapon," said Rachel, coming up behind me, teasing me with a smile.

"The only thing we know about this spanner is that Dylan opened his beer bottles with it."

At home, we spent several hours nest building with the puppy, then went to the pub for dinner. Ringle the coxswain was behind the bar, and warned us not to expect too much from O'Malley, only scrambled eggs and smoked salmon, which sounded good to us. We could hear O'Malley in the kitchen but he sounded less than his usual ebullient self. "Shagged out," explained Ringle, "been down the tennis courts." You have to be careful in west Wales if you're told someone's been playing tennis; it's how local people refer to the giving and taking of bribes. Sometimes they talk about an outing to Wimbledon. In either case, they mean back-handers.

"Tennis?" I asked tentatively.

"Sponsored match for Barnardos, a new community project in New Quay."

O'Malley was a fanatic for supporting children's charities. Over the years he'd taken part in some amazing fund-raising events, including making a one-legged parachute jump, eating sixty boiled eggs in an hour and speaking English non-stop for three days. We knew that O'Malley's father had walked out on him, weeks after he'd been born. "What was his mother like?" I asked Ringle. A sociologist can never stop being nosey.

"Not much cop."

"Brought him up badly?"

"Didn't bring him up at all. Handed him over to his grandmother when he was six."

"To look after him?"

"His Granny did fine to begin with, then the booze got her. Had to sell the house they lived in, to pay for the drinking. They went into a one-room flat, near the steelworks. She started working the boys in the blast furnace, just to pay for the drink. She sent him round the works, looking for trade, and she'd have them in the shed behind the slag heap, while he stood outside."

"How old was he?"

"About eleven," said O'Malley, emerging from the kitchen, carrying a plate of artichoke and palm hearts. He put them on the counter in front of Rachel, and put his arm round Ringle's waist.

"Someone reported her to the NSPCC. I was in care for years. Army catering corps after that, and the rest you know."

Ringle had tears in his eyes. He turned and gave O'Malley a big hug.

"Any news on the Stillness case?" I asked, feeling a little embarrassed.

"They've taken Les Prop-Forward in for questioning," he replied, looking down over Ringle's shoulder, a bald gargoyle stranded for a moment on the collar bone of love.

Les was the odd-job man around the village, retired early from working on the farms because the farmers had become fed up with his going to the Crown in Aberaeron every lunch time and evening. It wasn't the drink he was after, but the landlady. For ten years he had stood resolutely at the bar, never moving from opening to closing time, trying to win her affections. Hence his nickname. One night, she stumbled down the cellar steps. Les tried to resuscitate her, and that was the closest he'd ever come to the kiss he had so diligently courted, though it is doubtful that she felt the touch of his lips. Her neck had been broken and she died in hospital the following day. I couldn't quite see him as Ogmore Stillness' murderer. I felt a small surge of guilt, and heard Cressida Lovewhich saying: "And now you're subjecting an innocent man to the trauma of police questioning."

★ ★ ★

We came home from the pub, tired and looking forward to slumping in front of the television. We found a house full of protests from a puppy mad at having been left alone. Bedwen had chewed the bottom of the fridge door, overturned the waste paper bins in every room and had climbed onto my desk to do her business on the keyboard. We cleared up and while Rachel went to the kitchen to make coffee, I fell asleep on the settee, with a chastened Bedwen cwched in across my lap. I was woken by the phone ringing, and I skipped like a stone into consciousness, sweating wet from a bottled Brains nightmare.

I had been travelling on a plane to a mansion called Gelli where Dylan Thomas had promised to cook me a curry underneath the yew tree. I had pushed the overhead button to call a cabin steward to radio ahead to tell Dylan that I didn't like prawns, but a huge Brahma bull came snorting down the aisle. I screamed. Someone from a seat behind touched me on the shoulder: "Leave this to me." A nun came forward, carrying a red umbrella. She wore a tube-like coif that came so far forward that her features were invisible. She clucked soothingly at the bull, and then gradually manoeuvred it back down the aisle with the point of the umbrella, until it disappeared into the service area.

I climbed out of the settee, upending Bedwen onto the floor, and knocking over the standard lamp that seemed to occupy all the space between me and the telephone. It was Cressida. "I've read everything you've sent me and more," she announced.

I was struggling to sound coherent, my head still full of a grinning Dylan shredding yew leaves into a spitting black pot, swearing blind they were only coriander.

"Most of us get through life because we know who we are," she said slowly. "If that's uncertain, then we have the King Lear problem."

"'Who is it that can tell me who I am?'"

"Exactly. Each of us needs a clear identity, to feel good about ourselves, and understand how we fit into things, self-purpose, if you like. If this is absent or weak, then an ego-vacuum develops."

"So we go around hoovering up affection."

She ignored my comment. "We all have an ego-vacuum, to some degree or other. That's why we employ ego-filling devices. We buy things like cars or clothes or paintings and we use them to say 'Look, this is me, this is who I am'."

"But if the vacuum's extensive?"

"If we have no sense of who we are or what our purpose in life is, then we risk a complete psychotic breakdown. But that rarely happens..."

"Is Rachel in any danger from Waldo?"

Cressida paused, and her reply made my stomach churn.

"Who in *Milk Wood* is a threat to his wife?"

"Mr Pugh, the poisoner?"

"No, not at all. He only wishes to kill his wife, he's nowhere near doing it. For Waldo, Mr Pugh would be a model of temperance. No, you have to look for a male character in *Milk Wood* whose wife died in ambiguous circumstances."

"Why ambiguity?"

"It allows Waldo to infer whatever he believes will give him identity and purpose."

"You obviously know who it might be?"

"Mister Waldo, Llareggub's rabbit-catcher. Mister Waldo the barber, herbalist and catdoctor."

"What does all this add up to?"

"The most important fact about Mister Waldo is that he's a widower. So Waldo's ego-vacuum can't be satisfactorily filled through identification with Mister Waldo until Waldo himself is widowed. But Waldo can't be widowed..."

"Until he's been married. And the bride?" I asked rhetorically.

"Rachel, perhaps. Now, we're not talking real marriage here, this is not the marriage of two minds, but a marriage in the mind."

"Why Rachel?"

"Waldo believes he's Jewish, and Rachel's probably the first Jewish woman of his age he's met. She's certainly the first who's taken an interest in him. She's a *mensch*, as it were."

"So first he has to 'marry' Rachel in his head, and then she has to die, so that Waldo can achieve a complete identification with Mister Waldo?"

"And that's where the ambiguity of Mrs Waldo's death comes in. How does your Waldo see this? Did Mrs Waldo die a natural death, in which case you'll have Waldo on your doorstep for the rest of your life waiting for Rachel to die. Or did Llareggub's seventeen stone barber pick up a silver razor in his pink fat hands and, creeping in the dark, cut Mrs Waldo's screaming throat? I'm sorry to be so blunt about this, Martin."

"You're suggesting that Waldo may believe he has to kill Rachel..."

"If that's how he believes Mister Waldo became a widower. Yes."

"So she's in real danger?"

"I doubt it. I'm outlining the worst that could happen. Mind you, if Rachel's in danger, so are you. Waldo's Jewishness could flood his ego vacuum and he could see you as a goy who's stolen his 'wife'. He may be driven to 'save' Rachel, to cleanse her..."

"Oh well, if that's all..." I meant it to sound flippant. Cressida's analysis was beginning to sound more and more implausible.

"If Waldo suspects that you know about the ambiguities of his own conception, if he starts brooding that you might well be able to prove that somebody else was his father, not Dylan..."

"How could I prove that?" There was a sharper tone in my voice.

"I'm not saying you can, only hypothesising that Waldo may believe that you can. If that's what he believes, then he may well feel compelled to stop you making such revelations."

"By killing me?"

"There's a lot at stake for him. If you prove that somebody else was his father, then his whole Dylan-based, Mister Waldo-created world collapses. His ego-vacuum will implode. For him, it may seem like a choice between your death and his."

"I find all this very hard to believe."

"There's another possibility," said Cressida. "Which is, that I could be wrong."

"Meaning?"

"That Waldo's ego-vacuum is not filling with Rachel or Jewishness or Mister Waldo or whatever, but its filling up with silence, and in the silence he's beginning to see his real self."

"You mean that going to Meetings is actually helping him?"

"It could be as simple and as beautiful as that."

"That's what Rachel and the Meeting believe."

"They may be right, I could be wrong. I've never met him, I'm hypothesising on the end of a telephone line."

"But who do I back? The Professor of Psychiatry or the professor of silence?"

"We could both be right."

"I have to do something. I just can't wait to see what happens."

"Try thinking critically for a change."

It was below the belt, but I let it ride. "You have a suggestion?"

"You're too close to Rosalind, you're not asking the right questions, you're accepting everything at face value."

"For example?" I asked defensively.

"I've been poking around, since you're plainly not up to it. There's never been such a thing as the German Helmet Call Off. The British Falconers Club told me that for nothing. And de Walden died peacefully in his bed of natural causes, not killed by his own hawk."

"So Rosalind embellished here and there, it's only detail around the edges."

"She's not in the Register of Electors for Ciliau until 1949. Where was she? What was she doing all that time?"

"Lots of people didn't bother to register in those days."

"Where's the proof that Merle Kalvick became a Quaker?"

"I accept Rosalind's word for it."

"Jews hiding in the Welsh countryside? A young girl from the East End pulls T.S. Eliot and Dylan Thomas? Howard de Walden seduces Florence?"

"Stranger things have happened."

"Have you checked any of it?"

"I have to trust her, I can't check every detail."

"You're over-trusting because Rachel's working on the Dylan letters."

"I admit we have vested interests..."

"...and I really don't believe Rosalind had it away with Eliot. He was old enough to be her father, and he just didn't do that sort of thing. Oh no, we can't let Eliot go down in history as Rosalind's lover."

"I think you're wrong about that."

"Rosalind's a great story teller. She's cunning and imaginative and you're completely uncritical about the story she's spinning."

"You're confusing the facts with the truth," I replied.

"I always thought they were one and the same."

"You may be right about the facts but Rosalind is telling the truth, her truth, it's her world as she sees it."

"You're one character in her story. So you don't know the plot, aren't able to see the wider picture."

"And Waldo?"

"I've already told you. It's too early to predict if he's a danger, the signs point either way. You're just put out because you want me to make a medical decision, to say what's 'wrong' with Waldo, to help you avoid a moral decision about going to the police."

"Anything else?" I asked churlishly.

"There's P.K. Bergstrom's thesis."

"Sorry?"

"He did a doctorate on the Oxfordshire poets. Went out to South Leigh to talk with people about Dylan's time there after he returned from Italy in 1947. They didn't really remember much."

"So why's it relevant?"

"He interviewed Bill Green, who'd been the village grocer. Not a good interview, but Green kept going on about 'Caitlin's coloured child in the caravan', a young boy apparently, but Green didn't say anything else about him."

"This sounds very bizarre."

"I rang Bergstrom in Sweden. He thought that maybe Caitlin had an affair with an American soldier from one of the bases round there."

"And what happened to the boy?"

"Bergstrom never found out."

"And what's it to do with Rosalind and Waldo?"

"Maybe nothing. But it's so strange that my intuition tells me there's a connection."

★ ★ ★

The following Sunday, Rachel went as usual to her Quaker Meeting. I took Bedwen and a copy of Dylan's *Collected Poems* to

the walled garden across the river. It had been built in the eigh-
teenth century, and had once had twelve gardeners. In more
recent times, it had fallen into disrepair, but was now being
restored with a grant from the Lottery. I talked for a while with
the stone mason who was repairing the wall, and then found a
seat on the upper bank looking across the whole garden.

Until a few weeks ago, it had been a no-go, never-come-back
area, a stinging, pricking mass of nettles, burdock, brambles and
coppiced trees. Its two acres had not been cultivated since the
mid-1950s. Now it was clear, flat and almost virgin again,
waiting for design and landscaping, holding out the promise of
being a new, democratic garden, made for children in wheel-
chairs. Yet as the wall around it has been repaired, the garden
seems to have turned in on itself, exuding not promise but
apprehension. The unwelcome smell of threat hung in the air as
heavy as balsam. Diggers, dumpers and tractors would soon rip
the ground apart, clawing back the earth, looting the top soil to
create drains and channels, special paths, willow tunnels, slides
and swings, new ponds and a small lake. Contractors will arrive,
jousting with JCBs, turning up their radios, shouting into
mobiles, and throwing stones at their empty cans of Lucozade. I
will be driven away by noise and violence, and so will the birds,
rabbits and hedgehogs, and maybe even the otters and badgers
outside the walls. The sea trout will tread water for another year.

I turned to the poems, and soon became absorbed in them.
The only distractions were welcome ones. A pair of mewling
buzzards spiralled overhead for most of the day. At lunch time,
the two parrots flew willowherb-high across the garden and
perched squabbling on top of the derelict gardener's cottage. And
not long after, a glossy black spot in the corner of my eye became
a large dog otter that had clambered over the fallen wall in search
of the mason's discarded crusts and broken chocolate digestives.

Then Rosalind appeared, carrying newspapers and a flask of
coffee. She sat down beside me.

"Rachel out quakering?" she asked.

I nodded my head, and closed the book.

"Waldo's getting a lot from the Meetings, just like Dylan did."

I wished I knew more about Merle's influence on Dylan. His biographers have said nothing about her being a Quaker. I found it difficult to envisage Dylan sitting in silence for a whole hour, or being comfortable with the Quaker dislike of alcohol. "I'm puzzled that he took to them."

"You saw what he said in his letter about it."

I recalled Rachel's interpretation of the Quaker references in 'Lament', though at the time I was a little sceptical. Rosalind must have sensed my continuing doubt because she reached across and took *Collected Poems* from me. "Remember 'Poem on his Birthday'?" She flipped through the pages. "Fifth stanza, last line," she said handing me back the book. "Merle's love releases him from darkness. In the next stanza he discovers God, rejects darkness as a way of life, and embraces light as a place. His predators, the eagles, are then laid to rest and, in the seventh stanza, he finds an unborn God within himself..."

"That of God in everyone, as the Quakers say..."

"With," she continued, "a priest in every soul."

"Anyone can minister at Quaker meetings, there are no priests as such."

"And on the very last line, he finds himself in the clouds, in a quaking peace, as he puts it, his open acknowledgement of gratitude to Merle and the Quakers. It couldn't be clearer than that."

We sat in silence while I searched for the courage to air the other doubts that Cressida had placed in my mind. I decided that there wasn't an easy way to proceed, so I blurted out: "De Walden died in his sleep."

I heard the crack of Rosalind's neck as she turned sharply to look at me. Her cheeks were red but not with blushing. Her eyes told me she was offended not embarrassed.

"I have to check the facts," I tried to explain in mitigation.

"A garden would be very dull if it were just filled with Honesty."

"I thought truth was indivisible. Is that naive of me?"

"Most things I've told you are fact – the important things are fact – but a story that's all fact and no colour would be awfully boring, don't you think?"

"And you thought you'd jazz it up for me?"

"Why not appreciate the help I'm giving you? Why assume I'm trying to deceive you? It's hurtful, very hurtful." She turned away and gave the dog another biscuit. "Oh yes, de Walden died in his sleep but how does that look? A bit flat? A little prosaic, perhaps?"

I felt some remorse. "You might have explained," I said.

"Don't you see? It wasn't any old death I invented for you. No, it was the aristocrat killed by his own falcon! It was a perfect metaphor. By their vanities shall they perish. Surely you see? The war had just ended, we had a new Labour government, it was the end of wealth and privilege, or so we hoped...the falcon was Trotsky, Lenin, Herbert Morrison...the saviours my father worshipped." Rosalind slumped back on the bench. She looked exhausted. She took Bedwen up on her lap, and stroked her tummy until she stretched her legs like a cat. She turned towards me again and said: "Did you find any other shortcomings?"

I decided it would be tactful to say nothing further about Cressida's doubts. But I told her about the malacca cane that I'd found at the jumble sale, with the tooth in the top, and the art deco spanner from de Walden's sports car. She was pleased that these at least confirmed what she'd been telling me.

"So Waldo's been having a clear-out."

"Mostly Eliot stuff, apart from the spanner."

"Waldo was so fond of it."

"I wonder sometimes about Waldo and the connection to Stillness."

"You have the whole story on tape."

"I'm not inclined to break a confidence."

"Or break ranks. We're in this together."

I was torn between anxiety and confusion. "Please explain."

"Telling the police about the link between Waldo and Stillness would be as preposterous as me telling them about the link between you and Stillness."

I choked and spluttered on my coffee.

"If one is going to be absurd about Waldo, then I could say that you had a perfectly good motive for killing Ogmore Stillness."

"That's ridiculous."

"Not at all. I could certainly make a story about it. I might say that you were worried that Ogmore Stillness would persuade me to hand over Dylan's papers to him. Heaven knows, I could do with the money. If I'd done that, it would have meant the end of Rachel's nice little project."

"But I didn't know Stillness was in literary acquisitions until after his death."

"Well, you'd have to prove that to the police, wouldn't you?"

My amazement was turning to anger, and Rosalind noticed. "Don't worry," she said, reaching out to pat my hand. "I'm not serious, I'm just trying to give you a sense of perspective. The trouble is that we're on the inside of the murder case. We can see only the connections amongst ourselves with Ogmore Stillness. But what do the police see? You and I and the rest of us here are simply asking who in the village could have done such a thing. But the police are asking who else in Stillness' life might have done it, and travelled to Wales for the purpose."

"It's hard to tell fact from fiction, wherever you stand."

"Martin, can't we agree on one thing? We are working on this together, aren't we?"

I nodded, though I wasn't indicating agreement, only acquiescence.

★   ★   ★

I arrived home in a thoughtful mood. I fed Bedwen, poured some parsnip wine, and sat down to read through *Under Milk Wood*, yet again, to see who else was in Mister Waldo's life. The answer was clearly Polly Garter, in whose garden only washing and babies grew, most of whom were Mister Waldo's. This gave me no comfort whatsoever, not least because the text reminded me that Mister Waldo was searching for an Eve-like woman, soft but sharp, with whom to share his bed. That description fitted Rachel.

It was at this point that I began to wonder if I was going mad.

Here I was, parsnip wine in hand, and only a few sips gone to mouth, wondering whether my wife's well-being was at risk because of something that Dylan Thomas had put in *Under Milk Wood* almost fifty years ago. In the parched light of an early Sunday afternoon, that seemed ridiculous. Its only legitimacy came from an old friend who was, as it happened, a world-famous professor of psychiatry. But might it be that her own judgement had become seriously impaired after her husband had been killed by a landmine? Was it possible that the awful tragedies that she had encountered in Rwanda and Yugoslavia were distorting her own clinical assessments?

We each had different objectives. Rachel wanted to publish Dylan's poems and to 'save' Waldo, to bring him within the care and nurture of the Quaker Meeting. I wanted to protect Rachel from the man she was trying to save. But what did Rosalind want? Certainly she wanted Rachel to publish Dylan's letters and poems but I felt in no doubt that they were a lure or bait to achieve some other end. As I was thinking all this, I experienced a wave of desolation as my situation became clear – I was just a dispensable player. Disempowered, as Cressida would put it. As I came out from under the wave, I briefly caught sight of the sky – could it be that Rosalind's end-game was to secure a Jewish wife for Waldo? In which case, I truly was dispensable. Even to think such a thing was preposterous, as if my rationality had been eroded by the wash from Llareggub's bow.

But could it be true? Was the woman who had been forced to conceal her Jewishness when she first came to Wales now driven by a need to re-assert it through her son? Indeed, she had been forced to conceal both her Jewishness and her relationship with Dylan. Now, in the last years of her life, she had chanced upon Rachel who was uniquely positioned to clarify both of these important elements of her life.

I heard Rachel park the car outside the house and I wondered again if these thoughts were nothing more than testimony to my own derangement. Not that I was organically mad, but that I was becoming so as a result of the events in which I had been caught up, beginning with the wren in the bottle and Waldo's eating of spiders. I was part of an unfolding story that seemed to be nibbling away at my rationality.

I opened the front door for Rachel. She looked exhausted. "No Waldo again," she said, coming into the house and inadvertently stepping on Bedwen's tail.

Over a very late lunch, she told me that the Meeting had asked her to contact Waldo to see if all was well. I must have pulled a face, because she asked: "What's the problem?"

"Couldn't somebody else do it? Maybe one of the men."

Rachel sighed. "I'm an Overseer, and I live nearest to Waldo."

If there's one word that might stop me becoming a Quaker that is it. Overseer conjures up images of savage galley masters whipping chained and manacled slaves; it was also the title given to the parish officials who administered the Poor Law. But indeed, in the Quakers, an Overseer is simply one who has oversight. Their chief concern is with pastoral care. Hence the visit to Waldo: an Overseer would take note of absences, particularly of new attenders, and would be expected to enquire discreetly why someone had stopped coming to Meeting.

Rachel tried to telephone Waldo two or three times that afternoon but his phone was engaged. In between times, I tried to explain some of the matters I had discussed with Cressida, but my brain was so blocked with anxiety that the ideas came tumbling out half-baked. Psycho-babble, said Rachel, as I expected she would, and she seized on the fact that Cressida had said there was a good chance that Waldo was being helped by his involvement in Quaker meetings. End of discussion.

Rachel settled down to work on Dylan's papers. I pottered around in the garden and then took Bedwen along the Beech Walk. We climbed up the hill and I sat on the pile of stones, looking down the valley towards the sea. The farms were shining in the strong afternoon sunlight. Our cottage stood out brightly above the river. I could just see Rachel on the terrace. Then she went inside. She came out a few minutes later and got into the car. I watched it pull away, lost it for a while as it dipped down into the valley, then followed it around the road to New Quay. It pulled up outside the entrance to Fern Hill.

No, I didn't panic. I called Bedwen and we returned home, walking quickly to eat up the tension that was growing inside me. There was a note on the kitchen table explaining that the operator had told Rachel that Waldo's phone had been left off the hook, and that she had decided to visit him. I was calm enough to know that I couldn't call the police because how would it be possible to explain that my wife was caught up in a possible dénouement of *Under Milk Wood*? Neither could I rush round to Fern Hill on my white horse because that would make Rachel extremely angry. And if Cressida was right, going round to Fern Hill might make matters worse because it could suggest to Waldo that he was in competition with me. So I rang Cressida. She was at home but she was about to leave for London.

"You did the right thing calling me," she said when I explained what had happened, "but I have to leave for the railway station right now."

"But I need help. God knows what Rachel's walking into."

"My cab's here."

"This is a nightmare."

"Do you have a mobile? Okay, give me the number. Start walking towards Fern Hill, and I'll call you back in a minute."

My mobile rang as I was crossing the bridge. "I'm in the cab," she said. "Let's start with Waldo. Why hasn't he been coming to meeting? Been ill? Busy on the farm? Lost interest? Not at all. He's stayed away to check out that they've missed him. So Rachel's calling will reassure him that he's valued and he'll be back next Sunday. Where are you now?"

"Walking past the pub."

"Tell me when you get to the farm gate." Cressida paused as the signal weakened. "I've no idea what state of mind Waldo is in," she continued, "and neither have you. Let's be cautious and assume it's fragile. We mustn't do anything that makes him angry with Rachel or with you."

"You make it sound as if we have a bomb to defuse."

"I'm at the station, hold on while I pay the driver. Are you there yet?"

"Couple of minutes more."

"Okay, I'm hanging up whilst I get my tickets. Call me in five minutes."

When I reached Fern Hill, I stood in the shade of a holly tree, next to the parked car. It was almost early evening but the sun was still hot. Midges were gathering around my head. My back ached with tension. I took out my phone again and rang Cressida's number. "I'm at the gate," I said.

"What can you see?"

"Just a gate for God's sake."

"Martin, please, you have to be my eyes. Now look carefully."

"The sign is gone."

"Which sign?"

"Loose dogs, no callers."

"That's encouraging, that's something in our favour."

"What shall I do?"

"I'm in the train, and I may lose you now and again."

"I can hear you fine."

"I want you to walk up the track, there's another gate I think you said."

I reached the second gate in seconds. I knew what she wanted to know: "It's been unchained but the dead birds are still here, or what's left of them."

"But no new ones?"

"No."

"Can you hear anything?"

"Completely quiet."

"No birds..."

"Nothing."

"That is strange. Just going in...." I lost her again. "Sorry, a tunnel. I want you to come off the track and come in sideways to the farm. I don't want him to see you."

"You have a plan?" I asked, as I climbed over the wire fence into the field.

"I want you to get close enough to the farmhouse to tell me what they're doing, but without being seen."

"I'm not a Marine."

"Regress, go back, it's cowboy and indian time again."

"I'm half-way across the field. There's a small coppice ahead, and the farmhouse is the other side of it. I can smell something burning."

"Any smoke?"

"No. There's a dog barking somewhere."

"What's that awful noise?"

"Jet plane overhead. I'm on the edge of the farmyard."

"I want you stay there, don't go any further."

"I'm going up to the house."

"That's too much of a risk. Any sign of Rachel?"

"No, the place feels empty."

"Just stay where you are."

"I have to see what's going on."

"If Rachel's in trouble you'll hear about it soon enough."

"Not if Pugh the Poisoner's in there."

"Your trouble is..."

"That I love my wife too much just to..."

"...that you can't stand not being in control. Sounds like a lot of unhealthy macho stuff to me. Rachel wouldn't like it."

"I'm going to have a look."

"It's against my advice, Martin..."

"I'm almost across the yard."

"You're risking a lot..."

"I'm underneath the window. I'm just taking a look inside. They're sitting round the table..."

"What's changed?"

"The table's been tidied up."

"Is the wren in the bottle?"

"Can't see. It's in the other side of the room. Waldo's eating, Rachel's talking."

"What's he eating? Don't argue. I know what I need to know."

"Looks like bubble and squeak with...Jesus!"

"What?"

"Kippers!"

"Anything else?"

"Some sort of salad, could be watercress, and a bottle of Guinness. Three different types of brown sauce on the table."

"It's Mister Waldo's food."

"Is that good?"

"It's not bad."

"Meaning?"

"He's in his bride-making phase. Why should he harm her?"

"He's getting up. I can't see him any more. He's back. Christ! He's got the wren in the bottle. He's giving it to Rachel."

"She mustn't accept it!"

"She's angry, she's really upset."

"Will she take it?"

"What's the harm?"

"She mustn't take it!"

"She will. She'll want to set it free."

"He's banking on it. She'll be setting *him* free."

"She's standing up, I think she's leaving."

"That bottle is the vilest thing he could give her. He knows that. If she accepts it, she accepts him, in his wholeness. That's how he will see it, an act of love, accepting the good and the bad."

Before death takes you, O take back this.

"She's taken it."

"Get home as quickly as you can."

I ran back across the fields, slowed down at the pub and by the time I reached the cottage I had regained much of my breath and most of my composure. I went in nervously. Rachel was sitting in the kitchen. The bottle was on the table in front of her. I stood at her side and put my arm around her shoulders. "Did he give you that?" I asked. She nodded and burst into tears. I sat down and held her hands.

"It's evil," she said, "but I had to take it."

"He knows you'll let it free."

"But it won't survive."

"We have to keep it alive," I said, trying to hide the desperation in my voice.

"It won't have any strength."

"We'll build it up. I'll look after it."

"Chicken soup can't cure everything."

"It mustn't die, for God's sake!"

"We can put it in the spare coop in the barn."

"You could take it back to him before..."

"No, it's done now. There's no before."

I brought my glass cutter from the tool shed. We took the bottle out to the table on the terrace and laid it on its side. Rachel held the bottom and I started cutting. "Why on earth did you go to see him?"

"It was pleasant enough before he gave me this."

The movement and noise was distressing the wren but there was nothing we could do about that. I was cutting as slowly and as gently as I could. "What did you talk about?"

"Dylan's poetry mainly. A bit of Quaker stuff. He wanted to know about formal things, how you joined, marriages, deaths, that sort of thing."

"Is he coming to Meeting again?" The wren was quiet now, as if all its energy was needed to absorb the fresh air that was rushing into the bottle as the cut grew larger.

"He expects to come next Sunday."

"Would you be willing to accept him after this?" I asked, pointing at the wren.

"What we *have* to do and what we want don't always coincide."

"There's that of God in everyone, right?"

It took almost an hour before I was able to separate the two halves of the bottle. I lifted the piece with the wren at the bottom and gently tipped it on the table. The bird came rolling out in a cloud of droppings and feathers. Rachel picked it up and stroked its back. There were tears in her eyes once more. "Must the wren die to save the hawk?" she asked.

Before death takes you, O take back this.

"Let's climb Cader Idris tomorrow," I suggested. "We've always said we should."

"Before we get too doddery..."

"Yes, before."

Fast Forward 3

The thirst is quenched, the hunger gone,
And my heart is cracked across;
My face is haggard in the glass,
My lips are withered with a kiss,
My breasts are thin.

The Inspector came striding into the room waving a piece of pink paper. The Sergeant looked up from the typewriter and wondered what was in store for her now. "It's a D33/CONT-FX," *said the Inspector, pulling up a chair beside the metal desk.*

"Yes, sir."

"Official notification of a departmental interest in an on-going investigation."

"Never seen one before, sir."

"From the very top."

"Cardiff?"

"The Home Secretary."

"What's it mean, sir?"

"It's come via Special Branch."

"There's a security angle?"

"I saw the Chief Constable this morning."

"I don't understand..."

"They've asked him to release you."

"Special duties?" *asked the Sergeant, thinking of the expenses she could claim.*

"They want you on Elba."

"Why me, sir?"

The very same question had occurred to the Inspector when the Chief Constable had spoken with him. Why the Sergeant? He just couldn't see what she could offer if the security services were involved. "You speak Italian?"

"Not a word, sir."

"Ever been there before?"

"Never been further than Chipping Sodbury, sir. My niece's wedding. Married a jockey."

"Know anything about Elba?" If something was happening in Italy, he thought, then MI6 was involved, and Special Branch was just a cover.

"Not to speak of."

"We have two mutilated bodies, a case of cannibalism, a slaughtered dog and Nogood Boyo has completely disappeared." Not to mention that respectable Quakers and Jews were mixed up in the case, and Napoléon, too, by the look of it. What on earth, wondered the Inspector, did they have in common?

"So why me, sir? Why drop a tiddler in a big pond?" asked the Sergeant, looking perplexed. "My auntie always said..."

Rising from the chair, the Inspector folded the pink paper into his pocket and walked across the room. He looked back over his shoulder and winked at the Sergeant. "And mind your rear end when you're out there."

"Sir?"

"Italian men. Surely your auntie's told you?"

At Death's Behest

Little and much had happened after Rachel returned from Waldo's with the wren in the bottle. My investigation agency started to grow, though often it was work that I didn't particularly enjoy like spying on cheating spouses or finding missing pets – Mrs Eynon Maesgwyn had phoned to say that her dog, a plump and happy corgi called Sam, hadn't been seen for days. She was very upset so I had promised to give it priority.

Rachel was meeting almost daily with Rosalind. Their friendship had grown, and often they seemed like mother and daughter. Rosalind was very keen to learn more from Rachel about Jewish cooking, something which was neglected by her own mother in the effort to hide their Jewishness. Dylan's letters and poems were assembled in a format that Rosalind liked, and a publisher was sought.

Dylan's shed had not yet been found.

The police were still looking for the murderer of Ogmore Stillness. O'Malley, who had at last proposed to Ringle, had let it be known that the police wanted to interview Les Prop-Forward for a second time, but there was no-one at his house when they called. Hardly surprising, said O'Malley, since he was with the gardening club in Spain. Not that they would see many flowers there, only the roses behind the ears of the topless flamenco dancers in the night clubs. No, he wasn't a suspect but one of the lads who hangs out on the square had indicated that Les knew more than he was saying.

The wren died after two days of shivering in the coop, as though it had too much air and space to live in.

Waldo came back to Meeting, as he said he would. His behaviour was normal and appropriate. I had had no need to call Cressida Lovewhich again. Rachel's relationship with Waldo remained polite but guarded after the incident with the wren.

Nevertheless, she and the other members of the Meeting were pleased with the progress he had been making. They genuinely believed they had rescued a soul, and perhaps given peace to someone who had experienced a lifetime of torment. I was sceptical about that. Whilst I no longer regarded Waldo as a threat to myself or Rachel, I thought he was using the Meeting to build a relationship with Rachel that was mostly fantasy. Between Meetings, he telephoned to talk about Quaker matters, and sometimes called to borrow a book or pamphlet, reminding me of an adolescent finding excuses to call upon his loved one. Rachel was able to accept that this was happening but felt it was worth enduring if it brought Waldo to the peace and security of Quaker worship.

The cat, however, was thrown among the Quaker pigeons. Waldo formally applied to become a member of the Society of Friends. Quakers form a very broad church. The majority of Friends are refugees from other religions, or travellers who have been on a variety of spiritual journeys but found no satisfactory destination. People become members because they subscribe to the Quaker's opposition to violence and war. Would-be members are also attracted to the Quaker belief in a just and caring society. But what of Waldo?

Most people attend a Quaker Meeting for several years before applying for membership. Waldo's application after less than a year was exceptionally early. On this score alone, it posed difficulties for Rachel and her colleagues. Then there were the questions about his past behaviour and mental state. These on their own would not necessarily be a bar to membership. On the contrary, here was a drowning soul who had been pulled on board a passing Quaker vessel and who was now declaring he wanted to join the crew. But a wish to join the crew was not on its own a good reason for granting membership. The person had to agree with the destination of the ship, and the values and way of life of the crew members. Being at Meeting was proving to be of great therapeutic value to Waldo, but this alone could not be the basis for allowing someone into membership.

I was at home writing a report for a neighbouring farmer who had hired me to find his missing muck spreader. Rachel had been out for a couple of hours at a special meeting called to discuss Waldo's application. I heard the car drive up, followed by Rachel's footsteps across the farm yard. Bedwen was already waiting to meet her. I opened the door, and the rain blew in, scaring the dog for a moment and lifting my papers from the table. She looked tired and strained, and I wasn't surprised when she said that they'd decided Waldo's application was premature. They would recommend he wait for at least another year.

Rachel poured herself some wine, and sat in the bath for an hour planning what to say to Waldo. He knew that they were meeting, and was expecting a phone call with the decision. I became more and more anxious thinking about Waldo's reaction, and at one point I felt tempted to ring Cressida for some guidance. Rejection is depressing, and I was extremely worried about how it might affect Waldo.

We ate dinner in silence. I cleared up the plates and Rachel went to the office to phone Waldo.

She was back within a couple of minutes. "How did he take it?" I asked.

"He said 'Thank you for nothing.'"

"Is that all?"

"Then he started humming."

"Humming what?"

"'Abide with Me'."

"Let me ring Cressida and see what she thinks."

★   ★   ★

Two days later, Rachel received a letter from Waldo, apologising for his churlish behaviour. He had been surprised and upset at being rejected, but, of course, he accepted the decision and would certainly pay attention to the recommendations. And, indeed, that is what duly happened.

He became a diligent participant in the life and work of the

Meeting and within six months he had signed up for a number of study groups on Quaker faith and practice. And then, out of the blue, came an invitation from Waldo, one that had been sent to all ten of the regulars in the Quaker Meeting. It came in a small lilac envelope. The paper inside was yellow, and bordered in black. The contents were unlike anything I'd seen before but Rachel said I didn't know my Welsh folk customs well enough.

> I, Waldo Hilton, am desired to act as messenger and bidder for a meeting of true minds on November 2nd next, the day of All Souls of all kinds, here in my house to have clean chairs to sit upon, some ale, turnips, leeks and not a little song. As is usual for us, meaning those who know verse from Laugharne and yet more from Talsarn, we will recite with knowingness the sad death of Dylan, Son of the Wave. A great many can help one, but one cannot help a great many, so bring food and wine that the least amongst us may dine.

The invitation caused great interest at the next Meeting, and Waldo, reported Rachel, was clearly moved by the joy with which people looked forward to the occasion. It wasn't just a Quaker do, he mentioned, but he'd also invited one or two members of the writers' workshop that he'd met at Rachel's launch. The evening, he hinted, would lead to a better understanding of Dylan's death. That single sentence made me anxious. I did not like the proximity of Halloween and a memorial party on All Soul's Day when police were still looking for the killer of Ogmore Stillness. Fates were being tempted, I warned Rachel, but she took no notice.

We spent the afternoon of November 2nd cooking. Rachel made leek and asparagus quiche to take to the party, and I baked some rosemary bread. Evening came with a flurry of snow, as the wind swung round to the east. Wrap up warm, Waldo had advised, and that is what we did. We drove to the gate of Fern Hill and decided to walk up.

The track was lit by a line of hurricane lamps that Waldo had hung from the trees. Along the ground, Halloween pumpkins with candles inside hissed as the wind drove snowflakes through the eyes of the yellow faces. Half-way to the farm house, we saw a cluster of lamps, with a group of guests huddled beneath. They were gathered round a table, drinking mulled wine from a pan kept warm by a small gas stove. We helped ourselves and expressed amazement that Waldo had gone to so much trouble on our behalf.

We walked on, now a party of six. When we reached the farm, we found the house in complete darkness but a line of smiling pumpkins directed us to a stone barn at the far corner of the yard. I pushed open the door, stepped inside and paused for a moment, trying to take in what was before me. The group behind pushed past to find the warmth, but they, too, stopped and stared, gawping like children. My first impression was that we were layered between two miracles. The floor of the barn was strewn thickly with daffodils and above our heads, moving like mist through the golden rafters, were hundreds upon hundreds of butterflies. To have daffodils and butterflies in November was impossible but there they were!

I moved further into the barn, wincing as my feet crunched along the yellow carpet. The atmosphere and layout was a little like a church, and I wondered how the Quaker guests would react to it. Rachel seemed as entranced as I was. She took my hand and led me across to the wall where, in a church, the altar would have been. But here was no altar but a *perllan*, a large rectangular board attached to the wall like a painting. At the centre was a red circle, with a stuffed wren placed within it. Ribs of brightly polished wood ran from the circle to each of the four corners of the board, in each of which an apple had been fixed. I grimaced at the wren but Rachel gave me a dark look and said: "It's traditional."

On each side of the *perllan*, Waldo had secured two flaming torches that gave the barn most of its shadowy light. Where the heat came from, I didn't know, but it was warm enough to take off our coats.

We turned round and looked down the body of the barn. In front of us, a few feet forward of the *perllan*, a round pit had been dug in the earth floor, presumably to hold a fire, because the bottom was covered in shredded newspaper. On the other side of the fire pit stood a small oak table with a *menorah* burning brightly on it, and a plate of small cakes. "*Pice rhanna,*" whispered Rachel, "or soul cakes to you." Beyond the table were two rows of nine chairs. Scattered amongst the chairs were little boxes, each covered with a blue and yellow cloth that bore the trademarks of O'Malley's embroidery. On each box, there were more soul cakes, as well as a sheep's skull with a lighted candle inside. Behind the chairs were two tables that were to hold the food and wine brought by the guests. Alongside was an old grandfather clock whose tick sounded like water dripping into a tin can.

It was now almost eight o'clock and there were eighteen guests present, an equal number of men and women. They were a mix of Quakers and poets but also a few local people, including O'Malley. Then Rosalind appeared, stepping quietly out of one of the unlit corners of the barn. She moved amongst the guests. Waldo, she said, was ready.

We sat down, both nervous and excited. Rosalind came to the front with a tambourine which she rattled and then flicked rhythmically with the backs of her fingers. Waldo came in through the door. He was wearing a white apron over his dark trousers, with a white ribbon tied to the buttonhole of his blue shirt. His black boots were tied with white laces. He had a bowler hat under his arm. He came forward to the small oak table, picked up a soul-cake and crumbled it gently between his fingers. "Share! Share!" he shouted, making us jump in our seats. "All Soul's Day! A share to my father for playing with words, a share to my mother for not being *frum*, a share to the children who have never been."

Then he paused and invited us to try the soul cakes. I thought they tasted awful, dry like sawdust, but I noticed some of the Quakers chewing away manfully as if they knew what was expected of a polite guest. I spat mine into my hand, and let it fall amongst the daffodils.

"On this day of souls, we stand half-way between Dylan's birthday, October 27th, and the day of his death, November 9th.

That is a significance that binds us here tonight." We waited whilst he crumbled a soul-cake into the fire pit. "It's no accident, of course, that 18 of you are gathered here."

At this point, Waldo stopped, gave a nod of his head, presumably at Rosalind who was in the shadows somewhere, and a shaft of light came streaming across our heads, illuminating the wall in front of us, just to the right of the *perllan*. "This," he said, "tells you everything."

The image flickered rather eerily on the rough surface of the barn wall, but it was plain enough to see without straining. It was a simple matrix:

1	2	3	4	5	6	7	8
A	B	C	D	E	U	O	F
I	K	G	M	H	V	Z	P
Q	R	L	T	N	W		
J	Y	S					

I'd seen this kind of chart before. It was based on a Cabalist theory that a person's name contained a code giving information about the person's character and their destiny. They'd worked out a system for giving names a numerical value, and in so doing decoding the information that they believed was implicit in them. I'd once shared an office with a personnel manager who used this system when she was hiring staff and, amazingly, she was almost always right.

"We use the chart," continued Waldo, "to determine a person's name-number. Simply add the numbers for each letter of the person's full name, then add the digits of the resulting number, and carry on doing this until the addition gives you a number below 10. In Dylan's case, the numbers for his name, including Marlais, add up to 54, which in turn add up to 9, a name-number associated with achievement, inspiration and spirituality.

"Dylan's life was largely determined by the number 9 and its various multiples, the most potent of which is 18, a number which adds up to 9 and is also a multiple of it."

Waldo paused again as the guests began working it out for themselves, and after a few moments there was agreement that Dylan's name-number was indeed 9. I calculated Waldo's. It was 1, a name-number associated with aggression, action, purpose and cunning.

"Dylan was born on one of the most powerful 9-days of the month – 27. It both adds up to, and is divisible by, 9.

"Dylan's first poem was published on the 18th of May, his first collection contained 18 poems and was published on the 18th of December. His first nation-wide radio appearance was on the 18th of October, and his television debut on April 9th. Incidentally, that first poem was 'And death shall have no dominion', a line taken from Romans 6:9. It has 3 stanzas each of 9 lines. This was the first and only time Dylan would use that arrangement.

"We would expect certain compounds of 9 to have a special significance. For example, its square root, 3. Dylan and Caitlin had 3 children, he had 3 important lovers in his life, there were 3 collections of poetry, excluding *The Map of Love* which was a hybrid, 3 completed trips to America, and 3 houses at Laugharne."

"And don't forget the 3 kisses for his mother the last time he left for America," shouted O'Malley, much to everyone's surprise, but Waldo seemed pleased that we were getting into the swing of it.

"Let's consider September, the 9th month of the year, and made up of 9 letters. No other month does that, so September has a special status in the occult. It's certainly a creative month for Dylan – his second and third poems to be published came out in September, as did his second collection, *Twenty-Five Poems*. It was in September that *Portrait of the Artist as a Young Dog* was published in America, and in September that Dylan started work for Strand Films."

This was the first time that Waldo had explicitly mentioned the occult. I had wondered about it when I first saw the sheep's skulls with the candles inside. It didn't make me nervous, just more alert to what Waldo was saying and what was going on around me. The Quakers didn't seem fazed by it so perhaps I was being a little over-sensitive. On the other hand, I didn't think the Quakers would remain so laid back if Waldo edged over into other aspects of the occult. A ritual slaughter, for example.

"With 9 as your name-number, September will bring change, disturbance and upheaval. And that's exactly what happened to Dylan. He made almost all of his major house moves in September. Perhaps the most significant of these was to Majoda, an address made up of the names of 3 children. Dylan moved there in the 9th month of 1944, a year that adds up to 18, is divisible exactly by nine, and the result, 216, adds up to 9. There could be no more powerful combination of numbers. Precisely 6 months later, on the 6th day of the 3rd month, William Killick fired his machine gun through the kitchen window of Majoda. When your name-number's 9, there can be no more ominous portent than its inversion, the number 6."

I could sense that rest of the guests were as intrigued as I was by this series of coincidences, though I am sure that Waldo would not have used that word to describe them. Out of the corner of my eye I saw Rosalind move again into the shadows at the rear of the barn. I heard a quiet click as if something were being opened, and then an explosion of noise behind us. People jumped in their seats in surprise, and gasped with delight as white doves flew across the barn and circled in the beams above Waldo's head. I knew without counting that there were 18 of them.

"Let's look at Dylan's death," continued Waldo, "The most significant fact is that Dylan left Laugharne for America on October 9th. You will, by now, appreciate the importance of the number. He stayed for over a week in London, and arrived in New York on the 19th. He spent a few pleasant days socialising and recovering from the plane journey. Then things began to go badly wrong:

"October 22nd: exactly 9 days to Halloween, and exactly 9 days since Dylan finished the script of *Under Milk Wood*. He meets Liz Reitell, his American organiser, producer, secretary and lover. They have dinner at Herdts. This was the last proper meal that Dylan was to eat. They leave the restaurant separately. Where did Dylan go to? With whom did he spend the night? Nobody's yet been able to tell us, though it's the most critical night of Dylan's life, and death.

"October 23rd: Dylan's world begins to fall apart. He starts drinking heavily and taking drugs. What on earth happened the night before?

"October 24th: Dr Milton Feltenstein is called and, without doing blood or urine tests, gives Dylan an injection of cortisone and a prescription for benzedrine. Heap bad medicine for a diabetic.

"October 27th: Dylan's birthday, a day of depression and tears, his 39th year to hell.

"October 31st. Halloween. Dylan is seen drinking lager, beer, whisky and taking benzedrine. He does more of the same on November 1st and wakes up on the 2nd. with a massive hangover, unable to get out of bed.

"November 3rd: Presidential Election Day. Eisenhower or Stevenson? A new American future? Dylan stays sober all day, and signs a contract with Felix Gerstman for a $1,000 a week for lecture tours. He goes back to his hotel to bed. He breaks down, he weeps and talks in a maudlin way about Caitlin. At two in the morning, he jumps out of bed demanding a drink. He's back at 3-30, boasting he's drunk 18 whiskies, American size. Impossible, but he's been on the benzedrine again, still no food since October 22nd, and he's a diabetic, remember, a diabetic.

"November 4th: Dylan wakes up and says he's suffocating. Feltenstein is called. He gives Dylan the first of 3 injections of morphine and cortisone, fatal to anyone with diabetes, and Dylan goes into an irreversible coma. He's taken to St. Vincent's Hospital. It's a Catholic hospital. It's a charity hospital. No health service in America, remember. And the country's pre-occupied with the casualties from Korea."

Waldo stopped and the barn was totally silent except for the ticking of the grandfather clock. He bent forward, opened a little drawer in the table and took out a knife. The blade caught the flames of the torches, sending splinters of yellow light across the faces of the guests. Rosalind came forward with a basket of fruit. Waldo picked out an apple and a lemon. He sliced each into 9 segments and threw them into the fire pit. He turned to address us once more: "Let's go back a bit, to that night of October 22nd. Who did Dylan spend the night with? Who and what started the terminal slide?"

Waldo paused and handed out a sheet of paper to each of the guests. It was a photocopy of the inside cover of a book. The inscription read: "To Al, with best wishes, Dylan Thomas. October 22nd 1953." Underneath were a couple of signatures and the stamp of a Miami law firm.

"We can be sure of one thing," continued Waldo. "Wherever Dylan went that night he would have taken a taxi but how to find the driver? I have a small trust fund in New York. I have drawn upon it over the years to employ a detective agency to find him."

The guests looked astonished that this strange man from a little farm in Ciliau Aeron had access to money in America. I relished the irony that Waldo had used Eliot's money to untangle a mystery about Dylan.

"After more than ten years of searching, we tracked him down to a retirement complex in Florida. His name is Alayne Withers. You each have a photocopy of the autograph that he obtained from Dylan. It has been authenticated by a leading firm of Miami lawyers. We have a sworn statement from Mr Withers that he was the driver who picked up Dylan at Herdt's restaurant, and that he took him to Merle Kalvick's apartment.

"Dylan spent the night with her. He told her he planned to stay in America, and suggested that they might try to make a life together. His relationship with Caitlin was already dead, and, indeed, a letter was on its way from her to confirm this, but he was never to read it. His security in America was guaranteed by the contract with Gerstman. Merle agreed and after she had fallen asleep, Dylan wrote his final letter to Rosalind, telling her what he planned, and enclosing what would be the very last poem he was to write. He stayed up to watch the sun rising over the city, and called up the janitor to take the letter away for posting.

"When Merle sat down for breakfast, she told Dylan she had changed her mind. She had already made one bad marriage, divorcing within a year, and was not prepared yet to take on another serious relationship. Dylan was distraught. He left her apartment to keep an appointment with Liz Reitell at a seafood restaurant. He was distressed and angry, as well he might be, and refused to eat any food. It was at that point, after his rejection by Merle and knowing it was all over with Caitlin, that his mind and body began to collapse.

"On October 25, the relationship with Reitell also broke up. Thus Dylan was left alone, without any of the women he loved and so much depended upon. He was on his own in New York, thousands of miles from his beloved Laugharne. His props were gone, except the booze and the benzedrine. The rest you know.

"Dylan died in his 39th year – his name-number and its square root – on the 9th day of the month in a year, 1953, which adds up to 18, and divides exactly by 9. He died exactly 18 days after meeting Merle in her apartment."

I must admit that I was impressed. I had always been extremely sceptical about the occult and cabalism, as I was about astrology and all the New Age variants that had sprung up in recent times, most of whose practitioners seemed to live in west Wales, self-seeking English refugees from the rough and tumble of urban life. But here was a totally convincing demonstration of the power of a name-number in someone's life. I knew enough about Dylan Thomas to know that Waldo's dates and calculations were correct.

Waldo went back behind the table and stood with his head bowed as if he were praying, and perhaps he was. The barn sat in a very Quakerly silence for almost ten minutes. It was broken, not by Waldo, but by the grandfather clock which started, for the first time that night, to sound the hour. It was nine o'clock. As the last chime reverberated through the barn, Waldo took out a sheet of paper from the pocket of his apron. "This," he said, unfolding it gently, "is Dylan's last poem, written in Merle's apartment."

I felt Rachel go tense with interest and expectation. It had not been amongst the poems Rosalind had asked her to edit. I knew she would be anxious to acquire it for the publication. "I would be grateful," said Waldo, "if Martin would read it for us."

He took me completely by surprise, not least because I thought that Rachel would have been a much better choice, and I could see from her face that she thought so, too. I went up to the table and took the typewritten poem from Waldo. I read it through silently a couple of times, and then started:

> *Held holy and scuffed between lamb and raven*
> *In the hour's grain, the self priesting synod hangs*
> *Solemn with the scope of still quiescent leaven*
> *And now it grows, grinding the wheel of fire*
> *That mills the circle, heart's icon ungraven;*
> *Vibration of the Pentecostal lyre*
> *Sings between ribs of silence, tongues*
> *The quiver of blood in the tautened lungs.*
> *They ride the updraught like a spark to heaven*
> *Risen in the furnacing haven of their desire.*
> *And I am left dumb and grounded, wrung*
> *In the diminuendo of a bat-voiced choir.*

I gave the poem back to Waldo, and returned to my seat. Some of the guests had started to talk amongst themselves but Waldo interrupted and raised his hands for silence. "Would the men please empty their pockets of money, take off your watches and remove any other metal you may have about you."

We all did this without question, whilst the women looked on in amazement at the bits and pieces that were turned out of our pockets. There were several Swiss Army knives, which were obviously de rigueur for Quaker men of a certain age. O'Malley had not one, but two, corkscrews in his coat.

"I'd like you to go to the woods – there are torches and wellingtons at the back – and collect twigs from nine different kinds of tree."

I led the way out, because I knew how to find the coppice at the side of the farm yard. Thankfully, the snow had long stopped and little of it was left on the ground. The wind was still from the east, but the farm buildings gave us some protection. We muddled around in the coppice until we were satisfied that we had enough twigs, though it was hard to tell in the dark. When we returned, the women were drinking mulled wine and eating cake. Rosalind took the twigs from us and separated them into various piles. When she'd finished, Waldo came across and set them crosswise into the pit.

He lit the fire and we stood around as fascinated as if these were the very first flames we'd ever seen. The wet bark of the wood hissed and spluttered as the fire took hold, and the smoke curled up into the roof of the barn, driving down the few remaining butterflies.

"In the old days," said Waldo, "they tried to cure sick cattle by throwing a new-born calf into a bonfire." He paused to pick up the poem from the table. He looked directly and intently at Rachel, and I felt that something awful was about to happen. I had a feeling that a little bit of the old Waldo was in the barn. "I wonder," he asked, kneeling down by the fire, and putting on a few more twigs. "I wonder if we could purge the power of Dylan's name-number by throwing this last child of his into the flames?"

I thought for a moment that Rachel was going to leap on him, and snatch the piece of paper from his hand. Her face was taut with anger and she stood poised like someone at the end of a diving board. But, thankfully, Waldo stood up and broke into laughter. "What a ridiculous idea," he said. "What a waste of a fine poem." He looked again at Rachel. "Take it. I want you to study it. I want to know if you'd like it for the publication. I'm sure you will, I'm certain that something can be arranged."

Rachel took the poem. She glanced at me, and there was no need for words. We both knew that Waldo was suggesting some sort of deal or trade-off.

"And now for some food," said Waldo. "A traditional supper for this time of year, the *stwmp naw rhyw*, the mash with nine ingredients, specially prepared by O'Malley." Waldo clapped his hands, and Rosalind came out of the shadows again, carrying a glass tureen. She put it on the table, went to the back of the barn, and returned with nine bowls. "The first round is just for the ladies," said Waldo, and I saw Rachel and one or two of the other women exchange disapproving glances at his choice of word. "All good stuff. Potatoes, carrots, turnips, peas, parsnips, leeks, pepper, salt, and especially for Martin, spicy sausage, sliced-up thinly, which I had specially sent from Italy."

Rosalind began ladling the mash into the bowls, and when she'd finished Waldo said: "And now for the surprise ingredient." He searched in the pocket of his shirt and brought out a gold ring. "It was customary to place a wedding ring in the *stwmp naw rhyw*. The girl who picked it up with her spoon would be the first to be married in the coming new year." He dropped the ring into one of the bowls, asked Rosalind to close her eyes, and then shuffled the bowls around until it was impossible to tell where the ring had been put. Then Rosalind gave each woman a bowl of the mash.

I have to say that both Rachel and I knew that she would end up with the ring. And so it proved, but I don't know how Waldo managed it. It was so predictable that when Rachel scooped out the ring on her third spoonful we burst into giggles. The rest of the guests clapped and whooped and made ribald comments. We both, of course, understood the significance and seriousness of what had happened. Rachel lifted the ring from the spoon and diligently wiped off the mash with a tissue, while she thought out what to do. There was now a certain tension in the barn, albeit light-hearted. Waldo stood pensively waiting for her response. I perfectly understood Rachel's dilemma. In our own private battle with Waldo, she had to reject the ring without rejecting him.

Even I was surprised by what Rachel did next. She went across to one of the Quakers and asked for his Swiss Army knife. The guests, of course, thought that this was a hoot. She returned to the table, picked out a stick of hazel, and stripped the bark right off. She handed the stick to Waldo. "My *ffon wen*," she said, smiling at him as if she felt some affection, which she probably did in her funny, Quaker, all soul-saving way.

He took the stick and started chuckling and then laughing, until the whole party was falling about, though they didn't understand why. "Just my luck," he said, "to choose a married woman."

Rachel stepped forward and kissed him on his cheek, which I thought was going too far, and wondered what Cressida Lovewhich would make of it. Then music came falling like dew from the beams overhead, and the atmosphere changed once more as people moved to the tables at the back to find the food and wine. I took Rachel aside and asked: "What's a *ffon wen*?"

"The white stick, sent by women in the old days to certain men."

"Yes, but what does it mean?"

"Get lost. Get stuffed. I'm not interested."

"And Dylan's poem?"

"A piece of deception, and I'm going to tell Waldo so."

She didn't have long to wait. Waldo was moving through the guests with every intention of ending up with Rachel. She was waiting for him, again calm and radiating warmth, what the Quakers call 'unconditional acceptance'.

"And what do you think of the poem?" he asked.

"The trouble is," she replied, "it's not by Dylan, and even if it were I doubt if it's good enough to be published."

I thought that was going too far, since the poem was clearly very good.

"I think it needs a little polishing. Why don't you come to the poetry workshop on Tuesday night?" she suggested, believing she was handing Waldo off, but at the same time keeping communication open.

As we drove home, I said: "I still think it's a fine poem."

"I know. And if he behaves himself, I'll make sure he gets it published somewhere or other."

"He looked very upset."

In Death's Dominion

One evening, about a week or so after Waldo's event in the barn, the phone rang. Rachel answered and hung up almost immediately. Rosalind wanted to see her urgently, she said. She left the house about nine o'clock. I woke at midnight, but she was still not home. I rang Rosalind, clearly waking her from a deep sleep. Rachel, she said, had left just after ten. I phoned Rachel's friends in the village but none had seen her that evening, though one had noticed our car outside the Scadan Coch.

I grabbed a torch and rushed down to the pub. The keys were in the ignition. The engine was cold. This time I had no need of advice from Cressida, nor could I wait for the police. I had no doubt where Rachel was, and I was determined to get there as quickly as I could.

The gate to Fern Hill was tied closed with orange baler twine but I vaulted over and began to run. I heard Cressida's voice asking what I was going to do when I reached the farm. But I was overwhelmed by the present, stumbling and falling over the uneven track, startled by grotesque faces in the trees. I noticed small things. There were no cobwebs across the track. A screwed up yellow post-it floated in a pothole. Small blobs of vomit lay along the grassy edge of the bank. Toads sitting in pools, waiting.

I reached the second gate, breathless and hurting with fear. A paper carrier lay at the foot of the gate post. I opened the bag and shone the torch inside. I could see a cucumber, and two hooves covered in blow flies. It's significance didn't strike me until much later, when it was too late, anyway.

I scrambled over the gate. A rat was sniffing at a squashed hedgehog. A shoe in a pool of oily water looked familiar. Another yellow post-it. A pen. A credit card. A badger snarled as I passed too close. Bats stitched and gathered overhead. The seasonal smell of decay rank in the chill air.

Another paper carrier had been pinned to a fencing post at the entrance to the farmyard. This one contained the bushy, ginger tail of a fox. I know what this is all about, I thought. I shouted Rachel's name and then Waldo's but there was no reply to either. A piece of paper pinned to the door of the farmhouse fluttered in the breeze.

> *The maggot that no man can kill*
> *And the man no rope can hang*
> *Rebel against my father's dream*

I pushed open the door, and stepped inside. I saw everything at once, registering every detail, recalling how the room looked the last time I'd seen it, noticing the differences now. There were gaps in the bookshelves, like missing teeth. The photograph of Dylan was gone. The pot of pencils was empty. Crumpled sheets of paper covered the floor round the desk. The chair on which I'd seen Waldo sitting, trying to write, had been turned to face the door. Monica Sahlin's painting had been slashed.

The air was thick with the urine smell of cooking kidneys.

The dried herbs had been taken down from the wooden beams. The mattress had been replaced with a bed made up with white sheets and a pale blue duvet. The bottles of stout were gone. The bowler hat was missing from the nail over the mirror. A smeared apron hung in its place. The table was covered in newspapers, stained with blood. A butcher's cleaver lay on its side.

I rushed into the kitchen.

A large stew pot gurgling away on the stove letting off sweet, sickly puffs of steam making me gag. The battered head of a corgi on the work surface, its eyes still bright. Bones split open with a pair of nut crackers. Pieces of red flesh and dog hair everywhere. Intestines slithering across the floor like great rivers. Blood dripping from a chopping board into the kitchen sink.

All this I saw, and then ran, out into the yard to the stone barn. I kicked open the door, seeing nothing in the flickering flames of the burning torches, shouting as I ran across the room.

Rachel was naked, spreadeagled across a cartwheel propped

against the wall beneath the *perllan*. Her hands and feet were tied to the wheel with orange baler twine. Her shoulders were strewn with daisies. A hammer hung from her neck on a silver chain. Carpenter's nails covered the floor. Smoke from the fire pit had blackened her legs.

There was no pulse. There were no eyes, just slits stitched closed with rose thorns. There were no fingers on her writing hand. There was no hair, just a crudely shaved skull and a lopsided wig.

A note on the cartwheel said: *Golden in the mercy of his means.*

* * *

The forensic examination of Rachel's body showed she had been poisoned, though with what remained unclear. A wren's egg was found in her vagina, and a finger, that was not hers, stuffed in her mouth. Her own fingers were never found. There were other mutilations which the police, out of kindness, refused to tell me about.

Rachel was cremated at a private service, and her ashes scattered under the great redwood at Tyglyn. I attempted to exorcise one ghost by returning Dylan's letters to Rosalind Hilton with a note saying that I would be happier if she completed the project on her own. The parcel came back a few days later, undelivered. Mrs Hilton, said Basset the Post, had left the village, and her cottage was up for sale.

Waldo was the main suspect for the murder. I told the police everything I knew about him, and handed over the tapes of the interviews with Rosalind that would link him to the death of Ogmore Stillness. The police searched extensively for Waldo, but he was nowhere to be found. He had completely disappeared from the face of the earth, or at least those parts of it where police inquiries had been made and photographs circulated. I gave them the address of the foundation in New York that had supplied him with money. I also suggested they tried looking on Elba. Neither led to anything. The foundation declined to confirm or deny if Waldo was its principal beneficiary; and the police on Elba seemed uninterested in the case. They had no record, they said, of a man called Waldo Hilton entering Italy or being on Elba.

I had spent months in misery and depression, weighed down by loss, police incompetence, and my own powerlessness in bringing Waldo to justice. Cressida continued to be very supportive throughout. Her work overseas had finished, and she visited me quite often. I turned Rachel's office back into a spare bedroom so that Cressida could feel at home. It seemed quite natural that two old friends who had lost their partners should find help in each other's company.

Then something happened that changed the way I'd been responding to Rachel's death. Late one afternoon, an express delivery van drew into the yard, setting off the geese and the dog into a raucous turmoil of aggressive posturing. I took the small packet into the house. I'd been expecting a delivery of organic seeds so I had started to open it without any doubts about the contents. It was tightly sealed with brown packing tape that only the kitchen scissors could remove. I pulled out a white envelope. The words on the outside were Dylan's:

> *Light and dark are no enemies*
> *But one companion.*
> *"War on the spider and the wren!*
> *War on the destiny of man!*
> *Doom on the sun!"*
> *Before death takes you, O take back this.*

Inside, wrapped in tissue paper stitched together with rose thorns, was a shrivelled finger.

Waldo was not prepared to let me be. Leaving me in peace, leaving me alone to build a new life was not on his agenda. Rachel's finger was more a threat than a taunt. It made me realise that I was very vulnerable if Waldo chose to return. It felt as if the finger was pointing at me.

Before death takes you...

That evening, I decided to go to Elba. My intention was

simply to find Waldo and breathe life back into the police investigation. I was concerned only with self-preservation. I didn't think through the details or the dangers of confronting someone who had already killed two people. Waldo's package had made me realise that doing nothing invited far more danger.

Rachel's finger was also a wagging finger, accusing, reproving, reminding. Had I played any part in bringing about her death? Perhaps I should have taken Waldo's threats more seriously. I had been shocked about how passive I'd been as matters unfolded. It was learned passivity, Cressida told me, dating back to my childhood. Some children never recover from first realising how helpless they are in the face of events in the adult world. Rachel's finger said wake up! I felt the first heat of anger, though I had no thoughts of revenge.

Cressida was extremely unhappy with my decision. She thought it foolhardy and tried to persuade me not to go. But I was determined, for I was certain I would find Waldo in Elba. I travelled up to Heathrow, first calling in at the Public Records Office at Kew, where I knew there might be some useful information. Many of the confidential files from the last war were now open to the public, including some on the secret services.

★ ★ ★

The plane came skimming into Grenoble, sliding down the mountains on a sheet of cloud to a runway surrounded by rabbits. My plan was to travel to Briançon and cross the border into Italy on foot. I wanted anonymity and time to get used to the ways of another country. A couple of days travelling down to Elba would give me both, and polish up my rusty Italian as well.

To kill time before my train left, I wandered round the Arab quarter, bought some kebabs, and then took the *Téléférique* up to the old fort. From here, I had a clear view to the southeast, where the *Route Napoléon* cuts through the mountain. This had been the way of his escape from Elba, as he headed northwards to his final defeat at Waterloo. I threw some coins tumbling down the wall of the fort, and prayed for a more successful outcome as I headed south to the island Napoléon had so desperately left.

I arrived in Briançon in the early evening, too late in this tourist-filled town to find a decent room. Even the hostel was full, and the information office was already closed. I walked down the *Grande Gargouille*, thinking I might find somewhere in the new part of the town, down on the plain. As I passed the church of Notre Dame, someone hissed at me from the shadows. An elderly, one-legged man stood on his crutches in the doorway of a boulangerie. "*C'est un lit que vous cherchez?*" he hissed again. It did cross my mind that I was being propositioned but it was more likely he was trying to help me find somewhere to stay. He came rapidly across the cobbles towards me. "*V'nez, V'nez,*" he insisted, and set off down the hill, pausing occasionally to make sure I was following, and urging me on with a sideways sweep of a crutch. Eventually, we passed through a narrow gate in the wall of the old town. I followed him down a marigolded lane, with fields on both sides which were themselves surrounded by the new town sprawling outwards from the base of the fortified walls.

We came to his tiny house. He told me to wait while he went inside. Then a woman appeared in the doorway, his wife I presumed, carrying a folding bed that she assembled in the barn. I asked her about food in the town. "*Non, non,*" she grunted, as she stuffed straw into a sack to make a pillow. "*Pas d'épicerie, pas d'hôtel, rien, rien.*" Later, the old man came back with bread, ham and a bottle of local brandy in a bag clasped between his teeth. He sat on the hay, and told me stories about the Germans stealing his calves to feed the hungry battalions who once occupied the town.

I slept fitfully through the night, thinking of the next few days and what lay ahead. It was to be a return journey, a healing pilgrimage, or so I hoped. Rachel and I had spent the first night of our honeymoon in Briançon, walking up into the mountains the following day. It had been a marvellous time but Rachel had sunstroke and a pounding headache for most of the walk. I'd brought her diary of the trip with me, and it recorded that I hadn't been at all sympathetic:

> "Martin responded with a most uncharacteristic outburst: he was fed up with it; every day I had something wrong with me; there was no point in going on this walk if I wasn't strong enough; we might as well go back to London. All the way down the mountain I was a few hundred yards behind him snivelling..."

There was a lot to make up for.

The great long-distance footpath, the GR5, passes through Briançon. The next morning, I picked up the trail just below the *Fort du Château* and headed east, skirting along the river Durance in dark pine woods, soon part of a long line of walkers, all with little plastic bags dangling from their rucksacks with their bread and cheese inside. By early afternoon, I reached Montgenèvre, "a hideous conglomeration of tacky modern ski resort architecture", as Rachel's diary described it. Here the path turns sharply northwards to the Col de Dormillouse, and I said farewell to the group of walkers with whom I'd spent the last few miles. I sat in a café eating hot dogs and olives, and when the customs man went home for his siesta, walked down the road to Italy. I caught the last bus out to Ouix, another ugly, sprawling town given over to skiing but now empty, save for its residents who were out in full force for the *passeggiata*. I found a room above a pork butcher's shop, bought some salami from her and wandered down to the station to find out the time of the first train to Turin in the morning.

The journey south was hot, boring and noisy. The Espresso pulled out of Turin's Porto Nuova with almost every seat taken by Piemontese undertakers and their wives going to a funeral services exhibition in Rome. By Genoa, I was fed up with their boisterous good humour and got off. I waited for the slow train to Pisa, where I patted the tower and bought a straw hat. I caught the Locale to Livorno, and just made the late afternoon ferry to Elba.

In Rio Marino, I found the Bar Karl Marx, and told them I

was Welsh and that my father had known Aneurin Bevan. Soon I'd been found a room at the top of the town with a magnificent view of the bay. *"Che bel panarama, signore,"* said my landlady Signora Profetti, who warned me that there were 237 steps to the bottom of the town, and suggested I have dinner with her. She stewed some squid with garlic and vegetables, and told me of the time she had sung opera on the ocean liners to America. I wanted to ask if she'd met Dylan and Caitlin when they'd visited Rio but I was reluctant to say anything that might attract Waldo's attention. I just wanted to look like an ordinary tourist, interested in minerals, good food and the flowers of the *macchia*.

The next day, I bought sunglasses and a paper, and hired a moped which I left chained outside the shop. I strolled through to the harbour, and found a table on the outdoor terrace of Da Alfonso's, and decided it was as good a place as any to wait for Waldo. It had a clear view of the Banca Commerciale. If Waldo was here, he would need to come to Rio for money.

I sat in the café for five days before Waldo appeared. The time had gone quickly. There was enough to keep me busy just watching the locals and tourists going about their business. When the bank closed for lunch and siesta, I went off exploring on the moped. I also visited the museum and asked to see the script of *Under Milk Wood* that Dylan had written for Luigi Berti. I was nervous about this, in case it got back to Waldo, but it seemed silly to come to Rio and not see the script, if it existed – part of me believed that Rosalind had probably made the whole thing up. Yet I couldn't dismiss all she'd said – she'd known about the path that ran along the cliff from the watch tower to Il Porticciolo, and she was certainly right about the Bar Karl Marx.

The Curator looked nonplussed but took me down into the basement to show me a room full of boxes. Signor Berti's bequest to the museum, he explained, as yet unopened and uncatalogued. He could not guarantee that Dylan's script was there because some of Berti's papers had been pirated by the university in Florence. Still, progress was being made, and a committee had been set up to explore how the museum might fulfil the honour bestowed upon it by the late Signor Berti. These things take time...Yes, he remembered Signor Dylan, a kind man who gave the children chocolate and taught the miners "the English push penny" across the café tables. And Signora Dylan... truly a beautiful woman, very especial...

That evening, I did another stint in the café when the bank reopened, had dinner at La Cannochia, and ended up in the Karl Marx with the old comrades.

The bar was very much as Rosalind had described it. It reminded me of the salt beef cafés behind Leicester Square that were filled with photos of boxers, except that the Karl Marx was decorated from floor to ceiling with images of Communist Party leaders around the world. These were dominated by a line of black and white portraits of every Soviet President since Lenin. And, behind the bar, were the heroes of the Italian left. Gramsci had pride of place, with Togliatti, the two founding fathers of the Communist Party in Italy. Next to them was Giacomo Matteotti, brutally murdered by Mussolini's fascist gangs, his body hidden in a barrel of salted anchovies, preserving sufficient evidence for his killers to be brought to justice after the war. It was indeed a place of homage.

The back wall of the café was laid out with as much care and reverence. This was entirely taken up with a series of photos of AC Portoferraio, matched against various clubs from the Soviet Union, most notably the Kiev Iron Workers XI. The side wall seemed altogether more eclectic, with an assortment of photos that included Marconi, Sophia Loren, Verdi, and Gianluca Vialli.

I didn't notice Dylan's photo until late in the evening, when the bar had started to empty. It was tucked away above the lintel of the café's front window, and partly obscured by a climbing oleander. Carlo, the elderly owner, seemed delighted I was taking an interest, and immediately fetched a pair of scissors to cut back the leaves of the plant.

It was a portrait of a group in bathing costumes, signed "Webfooted Dylan, Porticciolo, 1947". Dylan stood in the centre of the photo, with Caitlin on one side, and a young and beautiful Rosalind on the other. Curiously, the man next to Rosalind was not Ian Fleming but someone I didn't recognise, perhaps a local, because he was deeply tanned. Even more curious, Rosalind was just as brown, unlike Dylan and Caitlin who had the blotchy patches of people on holiday who'd been in the sun too long. A little boy stood in front of Dylan, presumably Waldo, looking even browner than his mother. Carlo took the photo down, blew off the dust and polished it clean with a bar cloth. "You like Signor Dylan?" he asked.

I nodded. "A fine poet, a good Welshman."

"A true socialist. Come."

Carlo took me by the arm, and led me out of the bar. We went down through a dark passage to the back of the building. He ushered me into his living room which, like the bar, was full of photographs. On the far wall was an old oak door. I thought at first it was the way into another room, but then I saw it was screwed to the wall and hung some way off the ground. Carlo took me across. "My loved possession," he said.

The door was riddled with splintered holes, some large enough for me to put my finger through. Just above was a piece of paper that had been framed and covered with glass. It was a poem, and the handwriting was very familiar. "Door come from old *gabinetto*," said Carlo.

The holes, he explained, had been made by the Germans during the war. His sister, Francesca, had been out one day picking wild strawberries in the hills. She'd seen blood on the bushes and called some of the men from the Resistance. After a long search, they found a wounded American airman hiding in a cave. In darkness, they brought him to the town and made a bed for him in one of the café's outhouses. He was soon fit and well, and ready to be taken off the island. But the day before he was due to leave, the Germans raided the bar. An informer, said Carlo, spitting on the carpet.

The soldiers came crashing into the Karl Marx in the early morning. Francesca dropped to her knees, and managed to crawl out from behind the counter. She ran to the kitchen where the

American was making himself some coffee. There was only one place to hide him, in the space above the ceiling in the *gabinetto*. She dragged him inside and bolted the door. She sat on the toilet seat and he climbed on her shoulders to pull himself up. The Germans came down the passage. They shouted and banged on the locked door. Francesca refused to come out, the American was still not up in the ceiling. Finally, the soldiers opened fire.

They found Francesca slumped dead on the seat. The American had managed to get into the space above, and the Germans never found him.

"She gave up her life to save him," I said.

"No, Signor," replied Carlo, tears running down his cheeks. "She died to save family. If they find American, we die too."

I asked about the poem. Carlo gave a big smile. From Signor Dylan, he said, written after Carlo had told him the story of Francesca and the airman. He reached out and gave me a chair to stand on so I could read it properly. There was no title, just a dedication:

For Francesca i.m.

Because you said I must not lose it
Not the beaming moon nor noonlight
Spy out its place
Bedded on an untended grave
Weighted by sea-deep coral brain
Below the owl-perch stone

Loss-fear brought midnight madness,
Daylight named it rage
I'll climb the hill and fetch in flowers
You are not lost, only away.

Con sympatia, Dylan.

I climbed down. There were tears in my eyes now. "You weep for Francesca?" asked Carlo, putting his arm round my shoulder.

"For a friend," I replied.

"A good friend?"

"A very good friend."

We walked back to the bar in silence. "A grappa, Signor?"

I nodded. "The man in the photograph, next to Signorina Hilton?" I asked.

"Giovanni Chiesa."

"Who kept the hotel where Dylan stayed?"

"The same."

"And Signor Fleming? Did he take the picture?"

"The name I not know."

"He came here with Signorina Hilton in 1947."

Carlo looked confused. "Impossible."

"They came on holiday."

"On holiday? But Signorina Hilton live here in Rio many years. Why holiday?"

Now it was my turn to look confused. "But she came to see Dylan and Caitlin. They were old friends, from before the war."

"Impossible. They meet for first time in Rio. I saw it myself."

"In 1947?"

"*Si, naturalmente.*"

"Then who is this young boy?"

"Waldino Chiesa."

My head was spinning, reality reeling away from me, pulled by a gravitational force I didn't understand. "Giovanni was the father?"

Carlo gave me a pitying look. "*Naturalmente.*"

I sat down at the table near the window. Carlo bought me another grappa. "She was spy, working *al coperto.*"

"Under cover?"

"Si. Signorina Hilton, she came at start of war, dropped under *paracadute*. Special soldiers."

"The SOE?"

Carlo shrugged his shoulders. "She teaching partisans. Blow up bridges, stop iron mines, help soldiers like the American. Very brave signorina. Then she hit." Carlo grinned broadly, and drew back his arm as if he were firing a bow. "Giovanni send arrow."

"They were lovers?"

"Si. Next she was... ." He paused, and blew out his stomach as far as he could. "... *incinta*."

"With Waldino?"

"Si. She tells Londra. She must come home, she says, to have baby. No, they say, you stay. Baby good cover."

"And she lived with Giovanni?"

"No, he had wife, so she have room in hotel, with baby."

"Where's Waldino now?"

"Here, in mountains."

"Does he come to the bar?"

"No, I stop him, he always fighting," said Carlo. "*Un temperamento violento*," he added, tapping the side of his head with his finger.

"So what happened in 1947?"

"Dylan and wife come to Giovanni's hotel. She fall in love with Giovanni. Dylan meet Signorina Hilton here in this bar first time. Never before. She fall in love with him."

"And then?"

"Dylan go home to England. Signorina Hilton follow after."

"And Waldino went with her, of course."

"*Naturalmente*."

I thanked him for his help and kindness, and said it was time to go. He shook my hand. "You are only person never offer money for door of *gabinetto*." He reached below the bar, and pulled out a bulging file of papers. "Letters come from over world."

I glanced through them, mostly American universities wanting the Francesca poem. "I never sell," said Carlo. "Last year, Englishman come, not very nice."

"Tall?" I asked, "with two small children?"

"Si," replied Carlo, "and with very strong wife."

Ogmore Stillness had indeed cast his net widely.

★ ★ ★

The next morning I came down to breakfast early but by the time Signora Profetti had fussed in the kitchen and dealt with early morning callers, I was way behind my schedule for being at the café before the bank opened. Then, Signora Profetti started complaining about my "milk skin." I was, she said, "not healthy in the body." I spent too much time in the café. She implored me to sit by the sea to let the sun "crack the damp joints." Furthermore, she insisted I take off my trousers and wear shorts. Brown knees were a sign of inner peace. That I had no shorts was of little consequence. Her late husband had a drawerful and it would make him happy if I were to choose one.

I started the long descent to the harbour, wearing a pair of Signor Profetti's tartan shorts. I waved goodbye, and earned a nod of approval from Signora Profetti by moving out of the shade into the heat. The sun was already hot enough to quiet the caged song birds that hung from every window. The air smelt of dog rose, drifting in from the *macchia*, and synthetic lemon steaming off the white linen hung out across the narrow, cobbled streets. And at every corner, as I turned to descend another flight of steps, the blue blistering sea, as Dylan had described it, called me onwards, gleaming and sparkling like sheets of polished steel.

I by-passed the harbour, busy with tourists waiting to catch the ferry, and walked out along the mole, past the rotting jetty where Dylan had watched the scorched and naked miners drag the rusty trolleys full of ore to the waiting ships. Half way out, I turned to wave to the top of the town, where I knew Signora Profetti would be watching to see that I had taken her advice. By the time I returned to the harbour, the sun had already turned my legs pink, and I was ready for a cold beer. I stopped at the stall outside the fish market, bought a bottle of *nazionale*, and sat in the coolness of a large myrtle tree, watching the crowded ferry head out to sea.

The bank had now been open an hour, so I hurried to claim my table at Da Alfonso's. At the corner of Via Ginestra, I found myself caught up in a group of elderly women coming out from morning mass. The cool air from the church soothed my burnt legs and I was tempted for a moment to go inside. But the ornate interior seemed claustrophobic in its over-powering bad taste. As

I curved like a tartan porpoise through the shoal of black dresses, I wondered about the cultural consequences of celibacy. If the Papacy had allowed its priests to marry, the post-renaissance makeover of its churches would have been far more tastefully achieved.

★ ★ ★

The Ford Edsel stuck out like a sore thumb in a china shop. For one thing, its colour, a red and yellow trim with a spruce green roof, and whitewall tyres. For another, it was parked in the illegal zone outside the Banca Commerciale. I stopped on the corner at the end of the Via Scaligeri and watched a group of schoolboys giggle at the vaginal contours of the car's chrome radiator grill. I looked across to find my table in the café, and there was Waldo, sitting with two of the men from the lobster boats.

A policeman came out of the bank, pushing his wallet into the back pocket of his trousers, a Polizia Urbana, much resented for their speeding tickets and parking fines. He stopped beside the Edsel, and pretended to give it a polish with the sleeve of his uniform. Crossing to the café he embraced Waldo warmly, sat down at the table, ordered a coffee and started to tell a long story which soon had Waldo and the two fisherman laughing.

Soon the group stood up to leave. Waldo was much leaner than I'd last seen him. His hair was cropped short, and he wore a red bandana that made his hair spike upwards like cacti. He was wearing black overalls with faded tan cowboy boots, and a strange brass and leather belt that must have come from an Olde English pub. He crossed the road, and reached in through the open window of the Edsel to pull out some papers, before entering the bank. I ran down the little alley to the Via Magenta, and grabbed my moped from outside the hire shop. I jammed on the crash helmet and after two false starts got the engine going. No match for a Ford Edsel but good enough to keep me in touch.

★ ★ ★

"I knew you'd come eventually," said Waldo. I was strapped to a chair, the front of my shirt torn open. I'd tried screaming and shouting but, as Waldo had pointed out, this high in the mountains only the buzzards would hear me.

He took out a scalpel from its protective plastic sheath. "I think Butcher Beynon got it right, don't you?"

★ ★ ★

It had been easy enough to follow the Edsel from the bank. It wasn't the kind of car you could miss. I'd come round on my moped just as Waldo was pulling away. He drove out along the coast, and then turned west, taking the high mountain road to Vetulonia. I'd visited the village on my second day on the island. It was one of the few that had resisted the Elba tourist boom. It had no hotel or shops, just one restaurant, hidden away in the basement of a villa where Napoléon once called on his Turkish lover, a young man called Mulini.

Just after the village, Waldo turned onto a dirt road, climbing higher through the wild *macchia*. I pulled up, and watched his dust cloud track up the mountain. I left the bike at the junction, and started walking. I could see from the map that there were not many places he could be going to.

He jumped me at the shrine, a tasteless little grotto at the side of the track decorated with plastic flowers and solar powered fairy lights. I'd bent over to take some water from the spring, when he hit me across the back of the neck. I don't remember how he got me up the hill to the house, but when I woke up, my head aching with pain, I was inside and tied securely with leather thongs.

★ ★ ★

"I was going to fry Puss some old liver, but now I can give him fresh."

"You can cut the Butcher Beynon crap."

"It's my inheritance."

"Mrs Profetti knows where I am."

"Look, Puss." Waldo picked up the grey cat as it purred across the room. "A little martin's flown in for dinner."

"My brother's a policeman. I told him I was coming here."

"I wanted to spare Rachel, you know, but she said she loved you."

"You tortured her."

"It was a ritual, a cleansing, a simple purging."

"She wanted to help."

"We didn't have sex. Not my type. Nothing for you worry about there."

"She was trying to help you get better."

"Better?" Waldo threw down the cat, and came towards me. I screamed as he pinched out my nipple and sliced off the end with the scalpel. "There Puss. You can have the nice gentleman's liver next."

I felt the blood streaming down my chest and soaking into the top of my shorts. "You're Chiesa's son," I said, trying to sound challenging.

Waldo looked genuinely surprised. "My, you have been doing your homework."

"I've been to the Registry here. I know all about Giovanni."

"It was a long time before anyone told *me* about him."

"When you were young?"

"Much later, at his funeral."

"He left you the hotel, but you sold it."

"I wanted to buy Fern Hill."

"Things had gone too far. You were Dylan's son by then."

"She made me into something I wasn't."

"You don't know the whole story."

"Puss won't mind waiting."

It was clear that Waldo was going to kill me. I knew there was no chance of my being rescued but there was a hope of saving Waldo, sparing others. There was no American airman standing on my shoulders, but I could feel the weight of other lives.

"You know Rosalind was in the SOE?"

"She mentioned it once."

"When the war ended, they transferred her to MI6. They told her to stay on Elba. They wanted information on the communists, and Giovanni was close to the leadership."

Waldo looked perturbed. "She was spying on my father?"

"And the others. The affair with Giovanni was over, of course, but they were still on good terms."

"Torn between country and lover?"

"Yes, it's partly why they started worrying about her. The quality of the intelligence she sent was poor. They wondered if she'd been turned, if the Soviets were using her. London knew Dylan was in Italy so they asked him to stay on, go to Elba and bring her back.

"Dylan could be quite a charmer, and Rosalind fell for him straight away. Giovanni was no intellectual, and she'd missed that, but Dylan was exciting, overflowing with ideas."

"A holiday romance," said Waldo sarcastically.

"Maybe, but she followed Dylan home, with you in tow. Your fantasy father took you away from your real one.

"They cleared her, of course, and she stayed in MI6, probably became Dylan's handler. That's when she started to weave her fantasies. There was no harm meant, she wanted you to have some roots, I suppose. So Dylan became your father, and poor Giovanni just an uncle.

"And that's when the trouble started, wasn't it? She wouldn't let you write to him, or go and see him. She was wiping out the Italian side, filling it up with Dylan and Eliot. It's not surprising you flipped, became the village delinquent, especially when you found out Giovanni was your real father."

"I never understood the Eliot thing."

"The fantasising took over, she lost control. It was an occupational hazard in MI6, the plotting and counter-plotting, bluff and double bluff... they lost sight of their real selves, and the real world, too."

"Some of it was true," said Waldo, scowling.

I was weakening now. My energy was ebbing, flowing away

like the blood from my chest. The pain in my head from Waldo's blow was so intense that each pulse, each heart beat seemed ready to explode. Waldo's intent was now so clear that I could probably calculate how many more heart beats I actually had left. I thought again of Francesca, and the memory gave me strength. "Rosalind would certainly have met Eliot before the war," I said. "There's a photo of her standing with the Faber children outside Tyglyn."

"Dylan loved me, you know."

"He loved nobody, not even himself. It's Caitlin you have to thank for everything."

This time Waldo flinched in surprise. "Caitlin?" he said aggressively.

"Who d'you think persuaded Giovanni to leave you the hotel? She came back to see him when he was dying. Go to the Registry and see for yourself. She witnessed his will."

"Why should she bother?"

"You were the son of Giovanni Chiesa that she never had."

"I don't understand."

"The wife of your fantasy father was carrying a child by your real father."

"Caitlin and Giovanni?"

"And then an abortion, but she never got over it. She mothered you instead, did more for you than Dylan ever did, or Rosalind.

"When was this?" asked Waldo suspiciously.

"In South Leigh. When you and Rosalind arrived from Elba, they put you in the caravan next to the house. It was Caitlin who looked after you, when Dylan was at the BBC and Rosalind was travelling up to MI6 every day. Caitlin's little Italian boy, you were, the only one who knew the Lord's Prayer in Latin."

Not quite, I thought. More a nice Jewish boy bought up a Catholic in Italy, then dumped in cold and cheerless Oxfordshire, too dark-skinned for local people to be really comfortable about. Then spun a lie for the rest of his life about being Dylan's son, or Eliot's.

"Giovanni's will was the last straw," I continued. "You inherited the hotel and a bit of money but he insisted you went to Mass again."

"It was nothing, a bit of ritual."

"It was everything. A complete denial of your mother, your grandparents, the relatives in the Holocaust. For thirty pieces of Catholic cash."

I cried with pain as Waldo grabbed my ear, and twisted it round his forefinger. "No wonder you're so fucked up," I shouted.

He pulled the lob towards him and cut across with the scalpel. Blood trickled down my face.

"Say what you will," he said menacingly, "I still know how the Eucharist goes."

He crossed himself, raised his arms and cried: "O Lamb of God that takest away the sinners of the world, have mercy upon him."

"Wrong," I said, wincing from the pain in my ear. "Take away the *sins* of the world."

He stood silently grinning at me, holding a piece of my ear in his fingers. "Draw near," he whispered, "to receive the flesh of thy dear Son."

Then he leaned across and wiped the ear in the blood running down my chest. "The Body of Christ keep me in eternal life," he intoned.

He put the slice of ear in his mouth and swallowed.

I was sick, shooting vomit across the floor. The cat scampered across to lick it up.

Waldo put down the scalpel and walked to the sink. He washed his hands, and went down on his knees. "Almighty God, we thank thee for feeding us with the Body and Blood of thy Son, whom we offer to thee to be a living sacrifice."

He got up and came back across the room. "You see, word perfect. Did it disgust you? I'm surprised. I took you for a church-going man." He carefully polished the scalpel with an old napkin. "My love for Rachel was rather all-consuming," he said, giggling. "The kidneys were especially tasty."

I gagged again, but this time nothing came up. I thought of Rachel and wondered if she'd been alive when he cut off her fingers.

"Strange word, cannibal, don't you think? A corruption of Carribean, some say. Racist nonsense, of course. Comes from Hannibal, Dylan knew that. What else had the men to eat when he took them across the Alps?

"The people round here got rather used to it, you know. Times were hard in the war. Then there was the Liberation. The French army came in 1944, mostly Moroccans and Senegalese. Drove off the Germans, and then the troops looted and raped for a whole week. That's why there're so many dark-skinned people on Elba, though I wouldn't ever mention that if I were you. Anyway, the peasants came down from the hills and cut off the balls of the dead Senegalese troops. Took them home, fried them in batter and ate the lot. Good for the sex life, they said.

"Funny how people get the wrong idea about things. Take maggots. Wonderful creatures. Fisherman like them but nobody else does."

Waldo walked across to the fridge, reached inside and took out an old margarine carton. "Did you know there's over twenty-three thousand web pages on maggots? There's even an international maggot conference every year!" He held the carton close to my face. "Look at these buggers. Best you can get, shipped across from the Maremma swamp."

He put his hand in the box and scooped up a fistful of the squirming mass. "Take that wound on your chest. Could get a nasty infection, might lead to gangrene. In the old days, they'd put a handful of maggots in there, and in a day or two, you'd be right as rain."

Waldo smeared the maggots across my chest and rubbed them into my sliced off nipple. The pain was a thousand razor blades ground in my skin.

"They'll wriggle a bit till they settle in. They've got little hooks, you know, helps them burrow about in there.

"They'll just gobble up the infected tissue, and leave the good stuff. Debridement, the medics call it, posh word for cleaning."

I saw the front door open.

"Suppose you could say I've been a bit of a maggot. Took your bride away, didn't I, cleaned out the old marital infection."

A man came in, someone I'd never seen before. He walked slowly across the room to Waldo. "Debrided your miscegenous marriage, didn't I? Ate up the necrotic Rachel. And what thanks do I get?"

Waldo felt the draught blow through the door, and half turned to see who was there. He swung round and lunged with the scalpel but missed. The man grabbed Waldo's arm and tried to force it downwards across his knee. Waldo hit him savagely on the chin with his fist. The man staggered back and Waldo came at him with the scalpel again.

Then Cressida came through the door with a machete in her hand. She brought it curving through the air towards Waldo. He turned to fend off the blow, but the blade sliced cleanly through his forearm. Blood spurted out, covering my hair and face, filling my eyes, horse-tailing over my lips. He staggered sideways, his arm hanging loose, held on by a flap of skin. He swung at Cressida with his other arm. She hit him again with the flat edge of the machete. "You'll be dead in a minute if you don't stop that arm bleeding," she said coolly. Waldo spat viciously at her and ran out through the door.

"Time to take you home," she said, coming across to my chair.

"We must stop him."

"Old Chinese saying: man with one arm can't tie tourniquet. He won't get far. By the way, this is Bissmire Junior, Daddy's new driver, ex-paratrooper, obviously a bit rusty now."

We heard the engine of the Edsel start up. "He'll pass out before he reaches the bottom," said Bissmire, in such a matter-of-fact voice that I looked up in surprise.

"Go and make sure. Follow him down."

Cressida cut the thongs that bound me to the chair, and brought towels from the bedroom. I held one over my nipple to staunch the flow of blood, whilst she poured pitchers of cold water over my hair. "Let's clean up this room," she said when I looked respectable enough for Rio, and had a plaster on my ear.

"Were you going to kill him?"

"I had to make some pretty tough decisions in Africa," she replied, throwing me one of Waldo's shirts. "This was easier."

Cressida set about scrubbing the floor. I wiped down the table and chair, and took the blood-soaked towels outside. Bissmire was coming back up the track. "The car went over the edge," he said. "Gone up in flames."

We went into the house. Cressida had placed a half-empty bottle of grappa on the table, and was searching for a glass to set beside it. "Let's go home. I've had enough of Italy."

The track down was strewn with pieces from the Edsel, and a whole bumper had come off on the first sharp bend. Not long after, we found the break in the wall where the car had finally gone over the side. It had fallen to the bottom of a small ravine, and was still burning fiercely, standing end-up against a small cluster of carob trees.

"Bissmire and I will take the next ferry out. You stay and settle up with your landlady, say goodbye in the Karl Marx, just do the normal things."

"And the police?"

"It'll be weeks before they find what's left of Waldo."

"No reason for them to think it wasn't an accident," added Bissmire.

"Which is exactly what it was."

"One grappa too many on a treacherous mountain track."

★ ★ ★

We've been living together now for many months. When we arrived back in Ciliau Aeron, Cressida insisted she stayed until my injury was properly healed, and she has never left. I think she was more interested in my emotional trauma than the breast wound because she treated me like a patient who needed to talk things through. I resisted jumping onto her Freudian couch, but we got into bed instead and made love for only the second time in all those years since we'd first met. The only therapy I felt I needed was to shave off my hair, which Dai Dark Horse did on a wet Saturday morning when there were no fishermen pestering him for bait. But it didn't work and the smell of Waldo's blood was as strong as ever.

Cressida found a job, working with special needs children in the county. She learnt conversational Welsh very quickly, and even joined the local Women's Institute. I gave up private sleuthing, and started to write a book on T.S. Eliot and his connections with Cardiganshire. It won't be about Rosalind and Waldo, but about the poems Eliot wrote whilst staying with the Fabers in Tyglyn Aeron. I found a long-neglected archive in the National Library which shows that 'Burnt Norton' was inspired by Ciliau Aeron.

And then we had a baby, a lovely girl who we've named Rachel. She turned out to be the final block in re-building relations between Cressida and her elderly parents. Naturally, they were worried about the future of their baronial pile when they died. Cressida's their only surviving child, and will inherit everything. We haven't told her parents, but when the time comes we plan to turn the mansion into a home for war orphans from Afghanistan. This would be a much quieter revolution in the fortunes of the estate than Cressida planned all those years ago when she was a Communist.

Of course, all they care about at the moment is their new, and only, grand-daughter. They're already talking about private nurseries and prep schools and setting up a trust fund, but we've firmly told them that Rachel will be going to the village school, and will be taught in Welsh like everybody else. But we did accept a loan from them to buy a house. A new relationship, we decided, needs a fresh start. So we bought an old farm on the other side of the village, where we are now comfortably settled in, with all the packing boxes cleared away and the books in their proper places on Billy Logs' pine shelves.

Mother and baby were fast asleep upstairs, after a long and exhausting night. Having a baby in middle age is wonderful but sometimes I worried about whether we would cope with it physically. I poured myself a gin and tonic, and began to open the presents that had come for Rachel, most from Cressida's friends all over the world. There was one parcel from Spain that particularly intrigued me. It was addressed to "Baby Rachel" which I thought strange, because the name wasn't really known outside the family.

I'd started to take off the wrapping paper when Cressida knocked twice on the floor, the signal for a pot of tea. I took some up, clucked over our beautiful baby and came back downstairs. I found some scissors and cut away the rest of the brown paper, revealing a red plastic lunch box. It gave off a strange smell, pungent, like burning, yet sickly sweet, too. Smoked artichokes, I thought, sun-dried and dunked in olive oil and peppers, but what a peculiar present for a baby, though her parents would certainly enjoy it. I peeled back the lid.

Inside were the charred remains of a man's hand, and a black-bordered card that said:

Before death takes you, O take back this.

Stop/Eject

Disturb no winding-sheets, my son,
But when the ladies are cold as stone
Then hang a ram rose over the rags.

*The Sergeant knocked on the Inspector's door, and went straight in.
"There's something new on the Rachel Pritchard murder, sir."*

*The Inspector looked up with a welcoming but wary smile. There'd
been no progress on the case for months, and the* Cambrian News
was kicking up a fuss. "Sit down, Sergeant."

*She pulled up a chair beside the desk, and laid a single piece of
paper in front of him. "It's a fishing circular from Interpol, sir.
Apparently, our previously unhelpful colleagues on Elba are asking
for a little assistance."*

*The Inspector pushed the chair back from his desk, and nodded
thoughtfully.*

*"They've found a burnt out car up in the hills. Belonged to
someone," said the Sergeant, pausing for effect, "called Waldino
Chiesa."*

*The Inspector nodded again. It had come through his in-tray some
time ago but he'd given it very little attention before passing it down.
"Sounds more like a distraction than a new lead."*

*"They found blood traces in his cottage, and bloodstained towels
buried in the garden."*

*She noticed that the Inspector was hoisting his trouser leg up and
down his white shins, a sure sign of increasing irritability. "It did
strike me as odd, sir, that we've been looking for a Waldo Hilton who
may have been on Elba, and then we get a message from Elba about
a person called Waldino who's gone missing from there."*

"Is that all?"

"My auntie told me that Chiesa means 'church', and our Waldo is a Hilton, which is a hotel, if you see what I mean, sir?"

"Frankly, no."

"Giovanni Chiesa was Caitlin's lover, sir...I've been doing my homework, you see. And he ran a hotel on Elba. It's an odd coincidence."

"Have you looked into it?"

"I've checked Births and Deaths, sir."

The Inspector looked up in astonishment at the Sergeant's initiative. "And what did you find?"

"Born in May 1948, sir, in the John Radcliffe, Oxford. Birth certificate says 'Waldo Chiesa Thomas'."

"Not Hilton?"

"No, sir. Caitlin Thomas was the mother."

"So the father could have been Dylan or..."

"Most likely Chiesa, sir."

"And where were Caitlin and Dylan living when the baby was born?"

"South Leigh, sir, just outside Oxford, after they'd come back from Italy." The Sergeant looked nervously across the desk. "I went up there last week on my day off, sir. To see what I could find. We were sitting by the village pond when..."

"We?"

"My auntie and me. She was very keen to come, sir. We were on this bench, as I said, by the pond, when she noticed that one of the seats had a little metal plaque on it. Couldn't believe my eyes – In memory of Waldino Chiesa, 1942-1948."

"But you just said he was born in 1948, not died."

"That was Waldo Chiesa, sir. The name on the plaque was Waldino."

"So the man who's gone missing from Elba died in 1948," said the Inspector sarcastically.

"I was just as puzzled as you are, sir. A bit later, we went across to the pub for some lunch. My auntie started talking with some of the old boys in there. Apparently, Caitlin and Miss Hilton had gone up

167

to London one day to buy clothes for the baby that Caitlin was expecting. They left Dylan in charge of Miss Hilton's little boy..."

"Who was called?"

"Waldino, sir. Waldino Chiesa," replied the Sergeant with a quiet sigh of exasperation.

"But I thought Miss Hilton's son was called Waldo. He's the one we want for the murders, Sergeant."

"I'm coming to that, sir. Dylan took the boy with him down to the pub, and what with the beer and the darts, he forgot all about him. Waldino wandered off, fell in the pond and drowned. I've seen the death certificate, sir, no doubt about it."

"Then who is Waldo Hilton?"

"My theory is, sir, that when Caitlin's baby was born a month or so later, she gave it to Miss Hilton. Perhaps she didn't want it anyway, but maybe it was an act of love, sir, a recompense, if you like, for Dylan letting Waldino wander off like that. We'll never know, sir."

"So Miss Hilton brought up Waldo as her own, a replacement for Waldino?"

"It looks that way, sir. Easy enough after the war to sort out the paperwork – especially if you had the right connections."

"And the consent of the natural mother."

"I feel sorry for him in a way – he never knew who his father was..."

"And now it turns out that the woman he thought was his mother actually wasn't. We'll probably have to tell him all this when we collar him."

"I wonder how he'll take it?"

"I should think he'll be very, very upset. Anything else, Sergeant?"

"Just an odd coincidence, sir. When we were in the pub, one of the locals mentioned that somebody else had been in a few days earlier, also asking about Waldino and the drowning. A man with one arm, sir."

The Inspector shuffled impatiently in his chair. "Why should that interest us?"

"Arrived in a taxi with a little baby. Couldn't feed it himself, had to ask the landlady to hold the bottle. And she changed its nappy as well, she said."

The Inspector looked at his watch, and stood up. "Time to move on, Sergeant. Perhaps we'd better ask Mr Pritchard to come in for a chat about all this."

"I'd thought of that, sir, but his phone's been off the hook for days."

"Keep trying."

"I'll call round this afternoon, sir. See what's what."

With special thanks to Stevie Krayer for 'Held holy and scuffed', and Mary Overton for 'For Francesca i.m' (originally 'Witch Penny'). And to Mick Felton, Liz Welch, Manon Hellings, Siân Hurst, Andrea Bianchi, Silveana Siviero, and the Dylan Thomas Estate and David Higham Associates for permission to use 'Find meat on bones' from *Collected Poems 1934-1953*.

Written with the help of a Writer's Bursary from the Arts Council of Wales.

David Thomas is also the author of *Dylan Thomas: A Farm, Two Mansions and a Bungalow* and *The Dylan Thomas Trail*.